DISASTER
in the Yukon

www.zonderkidz.com

Requests for information should be addressed to:
Grand Rapids, Michigan 49530

Library of Congress Cataloging-in-Publication Data

Jenkins, Jerry B.
Disaster in the Yukon / Jerry B. Jenkins
p. cm. — (AirQuest adventures; bk. 3)
Summary: When a blizzard traps Kate in a remote Yukon community beset by dwindling supplies and an outbreak of illness, Spitfire and Dad make a dangerous journey to rescue her.
ISBN-13: 978-0-310-71345-6 (softcover)
ISBN-10: 0-310-71345-5 (softcover)
[1. Blizzards—Fiction. 2. Yukon Territory—Fiction. 3. Survival—Fiction. 4. Christian life—Fiction.] I. Title. II. Series: Jenkins, Jerry B. AirQuest adventures ; bk. 3.
PZ7.J4138Di 2006
[Fic]--dc22

2006006513

Art direction: Laura Maitner-Mason and Julie Chen
Illustrations: Dan Brown
Interior design: Ruth Bandstra

Printed in the United States of America

07 08 09 • 5 4 3 2

AirQuest Adventures

Disaster in the Yukon

Jerry B. Jenkins

zonderkidz

ZONDERVAN.COM/
AUTHORTRACKER

To David Van Orman, who wanted to go to Alaska and wound up in Abania.

Contents

Kate's Friend

It wasn't the news Chad Michaels wanted to hear.

"Suzie Q and her family are moving to the Yukon!" his sister Kate exulted one night at the dinner table.

Of course Kate would be thrilled. She and Susan Quenton had been playmates the first six years of their lives, back in Oklahoma. But that was five years ago, and all Chad remembered was Suzie Q as a spoiled brat.

"No kidding?" Dad said. "I told her dad Old Sparrow Christian Boarding School was looking for a president, but I had no idea he'd actually go for it, the school being so far into Yukon Territory."

"How far?" Kate said, her mouth full. "Will I get to see her a lot?"

Dad squinted. "Old Sparrow is near the Canadian border, at least two hundred miles east." He smiled. "I can't imagine Suzie Q in that environment, can you? I mean, those mountains, the river frozen most of the year, and snow, snow, and more snow."

"We all love that, Dad," Kate said. "Why shouldn't they?"

"Oh, *they* will," Chad said. "It's that spoiled only child who's in for a surprise."

"Chad!" Kate said, slamming her fork on the table. "You don't know Suzie anymore. She's not still six, you know."

"Come on, Kate. I'll bet she's still a dumb little kid."

"Now Chad," Dad said, "Kate's kept up with Suzie by email all these years, and—"

"And she's sweet," Kate said. "And wonderful."

"I'll believe it when I see it," Chad said, looking away from Kate's withering stare.

"How's she doing with her—what is it—diabetes?"

"Yeah," Kate said. "She gives herself shots every day. She says her mom is shipping a six-month supply of insulin up here before the heavy snow season."

"The heavy snow season is already here," Dad said. "Hope she knows that. When do they arrive?"

"They'll be at the school by the end of the week," Kate said.

Dad raised his eyebrows. "Something different for Hugh; he's been an Air Force chaplain for so long. But he'll do fine. I do wonder how Margie will do in this climate."

"Let alone Suzie Q," Chad said, shaking his head.

"Leave her alone," Kate said. "You've never given her a chance."

Chad smirked. "Maybe she'll grow up one of these days."

"She's already grown up, Chad," Kate said. "You're just too critical. How would you like to have to give yourself shots every day?"

"I'm not saying I don't feel sorry for her. But why does she have to be such a— "

"You have no idea what kind of a person she is now," Kate said. "Just be glad you're not judged by how you acted five years ago."

Well, that was true, but Chad wasn't about to admit it.

Dad stood and signaled the kids to help clear the table. "Kate," he said, "have Suzie Q tell her parents that I'll email them. We have to get you two together soon."

"When, Dad?"

"Soon. If we wait even until November, it'll be too hard to drive that close to Canada. Wouldn't surprise me if the Porcupine River is already frozen and snowed over."

That night before going to bed, Chad spent some time online keeping up with his sports statistics from the lower forty-eight states. Then he checked the saved email files to see what Kate and Dad had written to the Quentons. Kate had written, "Chad doesn't say so, but I think he's as excited about seeing you again as I am."

Could she really think that? No way. It wasn't like Kate to lie. Maybe she just wanted Susie Q to feel welcome in the Yukon or something. Or maybe Kate thought he was hiding some secret interest in Suzie Q. If she believed that, she couldn't be more wrong.

Kate also told Suzie Q about the wrist radios she had converted into wrist TVs. "They work for only about a mile, and the picture's fuzzy. We can't watch each other on our wrists from two hundred miles away, but at least we can play with them when we're together."

Dad's email message congratulated Hugh and Margie Quenton on the new assignment and said he looked forward to seeing them and Suzie Q again. He thanked them again for their condolences after Chad and Kate's mom's death eight months earlier, then added, "While it won't be the same without her when we get together, we'll have lots of fond memories to share. Don't hesitate to talk about her, as so many people around here do. I suppose they think it's too painful for me, but the truth is, there's nothing I'd rather do than think and talk about Kathryn."

Chad scrolled down to read the rest of Dad's message.

"We'll give you time to settle in and get your bearings, and then we'll try to drive over there the weekend after next. We'll leave Friday after school and probably see you late that night. The kids are out of school on Monday and

Tuesday, so we'll leave Kate there and come back and get her Tuesday afternoon, if that's all right with you."

Chad checked the file where Suzie Q had attached her picture. He was stunned. Sure, she had braces, but what a smile! What eyes! What hair! Then he woke himself up. It was still Suzie Q, the little brat. And he didn't like girls anyway. Chad shook his head and shut down the machine.

Two Fridays later it had begun snowing just before Mukluk Middle School let out. Huge flakes darted about as Chad and Kate helped Dad pack the four-wheel-drive all-terrain vehicle.

Chad had grown tired of Kate's excitement over seeing Susie Q again. It was all she talked about lately. She'd counted the days and then the hours. "Good grief," Chad would say. "It's only Suzie Q."

"Well, we've been here five years, and I've never made a friend like her."

The drive would take only about four hours, and Chad and Dad were planning to stay only one night, but packing survival equipment was their most important task.

People in northern Alaska didn't make a big deal about it, because surviving the cold and snow was a way of life. They got a kick out of people from the lower forty-eight complaining about zero-degree temperatures or even ten- or twenty-degrees-below-zero wind chills. That was everyday stuff for them from the fall to the spring, and when things got really nasty, they imagined outsiders just curling up and dying in the elements.

The family packed foodstuffs, extra clothing, extra boots, snowshoes, backpacks, petroleum jelly to protect exposed skin, first-aid stuff, and every other item necessary for survival in the arctic climate. They packed enough stuff that the entire cargo area of the ATV was full. Dad would have to use the outside mirrors on either side to see behind them on the highway.

The Michaelses pulled out into what was now a driving snowstorm. Dad drove the speed limit for the first hour and a half, but then the snow began to accumulate and he had to back down a few miles per hour. The big four-wheel-drive tires bit into the snow, and Chad felt as secure as ever. He and Kate turned on their individual lights and read as the ATV hummed along in the darkness. About an hour from the Canadian border the snow let up, Dad sped up, and they cruised into Old Sparrow County near midnight.

Old Sparrow Christian School was easy to find. Its buildings were the only ones on the north side of the road for miles, just beyond the sign that pointed east and said, "Old Sparrow 48 kilometers." The school and the dormitories were dark, but a light burned in the living room of the main house. Hugh and Margie Quenton greeted them warmly.

"Where's Suzie Q?" Kate said, looking around.

"I'm afraid Sue finally fell asleep waiting," Margie said. "But she insisted we wake her up the minute you arrived."

Kate looked disappointed, but Chad was surprised when she said, "No, let her sleep. We'll have the next few days together."

Chad was relieved to put off seeing Suzie Q till morning. When the Quentons finished going on and on over how much Kate and Chad had grown and how pretty and handsome they were, they were finally shown the spare room.

Chad laid out his sleeping bag, but as soon as he was snuggled inside it, his head near the door, he heard Margie Quenton burst into tears.

"I feel so bad about Kathryn!" she wailed. "It has to be so hard for you and the kids. How are they taking it?"

"Pretty hard. What could be worse than losing your mother? But we know she's with God. Heaven has never seemed more real to us."

That's for sure, Chad thought. To him, heaven used to be just an idea, part of a story. But now he imagined Mom there. He found himself often wondering what she was doing, what she could see and hear, if she knew what he was up to.

Mrs. Quenton tried to tell a funny story she remembered about Mom, but she wound up in tears again.

"I'm sorry!" she said. "This isn't going to work! I cry either way!"

"That's all right, Margie," Dad said. "One of these days, we'll talk about Kathryn without crying. Meanwhile, tell me what's happened with you three since we saw you last."

That was enough to make Chad drowsy. The last thing he wanted to listen to was boring adult conversation. He drifted off to the muffled sound of laughter.

Chad awoke when sunlight peeked through the heavy curtains. He didn't realize what had awakened him until he felt the door lightly brush his head. He sat up. In the semi-darkness he saw the form of a girl.

"Suzie Q?" he whispered.

She laughed. "No one calls me that anymore, Chad. Call me Sue."

"Okay, Suzie Q."

"Chad! So how are you anyway?"

"I'm all right. I was sleeping though."

"Sorry. I was just so eager to see you guys."

"To see Kate, you mean."

"Well, both of you, silly. Why not?"

Chad wished he could see her better. "You want me to wake Kate?"

Suzie Q seemed to think about it. "Nah," she said. "If she wakes up, she wakes up. I'll talk to you, if it's all right."

Chad shrugged, then realized that Suzie Q couldn't see him.

"I've been praying for you," she said.

"Really?"

"Course. Losing your mom and everything."

"Yeah." Chad squirmed.

"You don't want to talk about it?"

"I don't mind, but I like the good memories, not the sad ones."

"Tell me some of them."

Suzie Q sounded genuinely interested and seemed to really listen. Chad couldn't remember the last time he had talked so easily and casually with a girl, other than Kate. Could this really be the girl who gave him so much grief when they were little?

He told her the story about the time his mother had taken him out for lunch, just the two of them, on his birthday. For some reason, as simple as the story was, it made Suzie Q cry. He felt a little emotional himself as he talked about Mom.

"Well, Chad," she said finally, "to tell you the truth, I was always jealous of you and Kate because you had each other. Being an only child has its good parts, but it's lonely too. When I heard about your mother, I felt so guilty for any bad feelings I'd ever had about you. It was as if I grew up in one night. I was so thankful for my parents and so glad that you and Kate had each other. Can you imagine going through something like that without Kate?"

Chad just shrugged and grunted. As for Kate, he'd had lots of frustrating times with her lately. Every day certain things irritated them about each other. But to go through losing Mom without her? Suzie Q was right.

The girl in front of him had changed, all right. He could tell she wasn't just being friendly. Still, he felt awkward and wished Kate would wake up soon.

Storm Warnings

Their talking finally woke Kate, and she jumped up to hug Suzie Q. Chad decided this was a good time to slip away. He found Dad alone at the kitchen table, reading his Bible.

"Hey, Spitfire," Dad said. "The girls up?"

Chad nodded. "How soon can we get out of here?"

Dad snorted. "Suzie Q on your nerves already?"

"Nah. It's just that this place will be boring."

After a big breakfast, the Quentons had to sweep snow away from their walkways and driveway. In the harsh, sunlit white of the day, Chad noticed how Mr. and Mrs. Quenton had aged since he saw them last. They were a few years older than his dad anyway, but now he saw lines in their faces and around their eyes. Both were tall and light-haired with glasses and perfect teeth.

Both families toured the little compound where a couple of hundred kids from kindergarten to eighth grade lived during the school year. Many of their parents were missionaries to the Indians and Eskimos of northern Canada and Alaska.

Chad kept finding himself stealing glances at Suzie Q. She was as pretty as her last picture on the computer, but Chad tried not to get caught staring at her. He knew those braces would make her teeth as perfect as her mother's, and her freckles and long, strawberry-blonde hair almost made Chad forget that he hated girls.

"Do you have a CB radio in your ATV?" Mr. Quenton asked Dad, as the six of them trudged through the snow to the main buildings.

"Oh, yeah. You have to in these parts. Too much open space between towns. No decent cell coverage either. Can't risk getting stuck in the middle of nowhere with no communication."

"Did you hear anything last night about the weather that's supposed to be coming this way?"

Dad shook his head. "Truckers and people around here don't talk about it much unless it's out of the ordinary. Blizzards don't bother us much—"

"We heard it was supposed to be quite a storm coming in tonight," Mr. Quenton said. "A snow thunderstorm, something I've never heard of."

Dad smiled. "Pretty common. I'll keep an ear open when Chad and I head back later this morning, but I wouldn't worry about it. In fact, you'd better get used to it. The next six months are going to be mighty cold and snowy."

Hugh Quenton wanted to hear all about AirQuest Adventures. After Dad told him how the little family organization was born, Hugh asked Chad about their adventures. "I hear you were the hero in the Indonesian jungles and that you and Kate helped rescue your dad in South America."

"Yeah, I guess." Chad was proud of his part in both those adventures, but what was he supposed to say? "What sports do you have in the Yukon?"

"Lots of basketball and volleyball in the winter and softball when the weather clears."

Kate and Suzie Q ran off to explore and to meet Suzie Q's new friends. Mrs. Quenton left to check on the infirmary. Chad, Dad, and Mr. Quenton went to the gym, housed in a huge Quonset hut building. Boys' and girls' basketball and volleyball games were being played all over the building at the same time.

"I'd get you into one of the games, Chad," Mr. Quenton said, "but this is an intramural league setup, different dorms against each other."

As Chad sat in the bleachers behind his dad and Mr. Quenton, he wished he could play basketball, but mostly he just wanted to get on the road toward home. It would be nice to have Dad all to himself for a few days. He hadn't been alone with Dad for more than a few hours for a long time.

"I'm sure glad you spotted this job opening," Hugh Quenton said, and Chad leaned forward to listen. "I think we're really going to like it here. Would you ever send your kids to a place like this?"

"Not on your life," Dad said. "As happy as I am for you getting this job, I frankly don't agree with places like this. I mean, if the missionary kids have to go somewhere, I'm glad it's a nice place with good leadership, but what a thing to do to a kid."

"You know, Bruce, I agree with you. In fact, I told the mission board that when they were interviewing me. I told them they should take the salary they were offering me and add some to it so teachers could be sent to the remote mission posts to teach the kids there." He glanced back at Chad. "That way they wouldn't have to be sent hundreds or even thousands of miles away from their parents for months at a time."

"What did they say?" Chad said.

"They showed me what that would cost, but they also told me that someone with my view was the kind of guy they would like running the place." He ran a hand through his thin hair. "Margie and I have already tried making this place as much like home as possible. We brought a bunch of used computers with us after we heard they had broadband high-speed access here."

"They do?" Chad said. "Clear up here in the boonies?"

"Yup." He waved toward the students. "These kids need low-cost daily contact with their parents, and we plan to make sure it happens."

"Good for you, Hugh," Dad said. "Is Margie running the infirmary?"

"Yeah, her nursing and my seminary training gave the mission board just what they wanted. The place used to count on circuit-riding nurses and the occasional doctor from a clinic in Old Sparrow. This is good for Margie. She had to work off base in Enid because she wasn't military. We like working together."

"I noticed Suzie Q, sorry, Sue, doesn't stay in the dorm. Or was she just trying to wait up for Kate last night?"

"No, because of her diabetes we like to have her with us at night. We try not to baby her, but we can't take chances yet either. They tell us that this child-onset type of diabetes will stabilize as she gets older and she'll be able to regulate her own medicine better."

"She's sure growing up into a beautiful girl."

"Kate, too."

"Thanks."

Chad was bored again. All this stuff about girls growing up and becoming beautiful was making him sick. It was true about Suzie Q, of course. He could see that. And people in Mukluk all thought Kate was cute, but he couldn't see it. His sister?

A sweaty little roly-poly boy with jet black hair and a red face ran up to Mr. Quenton and thrust a note into his hand. "Message for you, sir!" he said.

"Thanks, Oliver," Mr. Quenton said, and he excused himself.

"Can we get going, Dad?" Chad said.

"It won't be long, Spitfire. Pick a game and enjoy it."

"I can't tell what the score is anyway, and I can't play."

"You want to shoot some hoops at the church when we get home?"

"Yeah!"

"We'll leave within the hour."

Mr. Quenton returned. "Margie says the infirmary is full this morning. Some kind of a bug. I'll have to go into Old Sparrow to get some antibiotics."

"You're out?"

"No, but we didn't plan on all twelve beds being full today. If we get any more cases, we're going to have problems."

"Why don't we leave early and pick up the stuff in Old Sparrow?" Chad said.

"I couldn't ask you to do that," Mr. Quenton said.

"Shouldn't you stick around here?" Dad said.

"Probably, but I could just as easily send a staffer."

"No, let us do it," Dad said, and Chad silently cheered.

"If you wouldn't mind, Bruce, see if Sue's medicine has come in too. It's a pretty expensive supply, but I'll give you a note and they'll bill us."

On their way out of the school grounds, Chad noticed a huge machine. "What's that contraption?" he said.

"Looks like a combination snowplow and snowblower." Dad chuckled. "Looks as old as the hills, doesn't it?"

"I'd like to check it out," Chad said.

"You stay away from that thing. It looks like it hasn't been used in years."

In Old Sparrow, Dad filled the gas tank and asked the attendant what the Christian school used for snow removal. "They got an ancient plow out there," the man said. "Makes more of a mess than anything, but somehow they get it to fire up when they need it."

At the drugstore Dad showed the pharmacist the note from Hugh Quenton. "How's that new president workin' out over there?" the man said. "Seems like a good guy. Former military, you know."

"I know," Dad said. "I used to serve with him."

"You a chaplain too?"

"No, sir. Former fighter pilot."

Chad couldn't have been more proud and watched for the man's reaction.

"You don't say."

"Anyway, Hugh seems to be working out fine."

"Well," the pharmacist said, "we're low on antibiotics, but I'll give you what I have. His daughter's stuff hasn't come in yet. Last we heard it was airborne, but you know we get our stock from Edmonton. They fly a route that takes 'em through northwest B.C. and then up into the Yukon. They have stops in eight or ten places before they get to us."

Chad whistled. "So when will it get here?"

"Supposed to be tomorrow. We'll get more antibiotics then too, but we got word last night the pilot's hung up in Whitehorse in weather and can't promise when he'll get out."

"That so?" Dad said. "Well, at least that weather system is heading away from us."

"Yeah," the man said, "but haven't you heard? Something huge is brewing in the Brooks Range."

"The Brooks Range?" Chad said. "Isn't that a long way from here?"

The pharmacist leaned on the counter. "Yeah, but they get to us eventually. Nobody's traveling in the mountains up there, so they say."

"They seldom do," Dad said. "I wouldn't worry about snow in the Brooks."

"You're probably right, but when you hear about weather that far away, it sounds like something out of the ordinary."

"Even for here," Dad said as the man bagged the medicine.

"Yes, sir," the man said. "Even for here."

Forty minutes later Chad and Dad pulled into the Old Sparrow Christian School again. The sun rode high in a cloudless sky, and the modest, rambling complex of buildings actually looked pretty and serene. Suzie Q and Kate were waiting to say their good-byes. Hugh Quenton thanked Dad for the package and the news and said, "Margie sends her best and apologizes that she can't leave the infirmary just now. She'll look forward to a little more time with you when you come back Tuesday."

"Tell her I understand."

Dad and Chad hugged Kate, and Suzie Q actually hugged Chad. He couldn't remember the last time he had hugged a girl other than his sister, and he froze. He just stood there as she giggled at his discomfort. "See ya," he said.

As he backed away, Suzie Q looked right into his eyes, smiling. He turned and bumped into Dad.

"Whoa there, big guy," Dad said, and Chad felt himself blushing. Boy, was he glad his friends weren't here to see this.

Chad had not slept well the night before, and he became aware of it as soon as he settled in for the long ride home. He lowered the front passenger seat and tried to stretch out, thinking this was at least more comfortable than the sleeping bag on the floor last night. But the sun was so bright he had to hide his eyes. And Dad kept the CB on the whole way to monitor the weather. So Chad didn't really sleep. He just rested.

"Hard to believe they're talking about weather when you see a sky like this," Dad said.

"Um-hm," Chad mumbled. He hadn't seen a cloud. It was cold though, despite the harsh sun. The windows were edged with ice, and the ground was snow covered, but it sure didn't look like anything close to a blizzard was coming.

Over the CB came a warning from the weather bureau, predicting that the massive storm over Meat Mountain in the Brooks Range would still pack a wallop when it swept all the way to the Yukon Flats, Alaska, by nightfall.

"That's hard to believe," Dad mumbled as he grabbed the microphone. "This is Fighter Pilot westbound out of Old

Sparrow, en route to Mukluk. Anybody seeing any of this weather yet?"

"Negative, Fighter Pilot. This is Fat Fox comin' at you from the west in an eighteen-wheeler. Lookin' fine from here, pardner, but there's also somethin' brewin' from the west."

"Repeat?"

"Hughes, that little town on the Koyukuk south of the forks, is buried."

"Ten-four," Dad said, then clicked off. "Chad, that makes no sense. One system coming down at us from the Brooks, and another sweeping east out of Koyukuk. They can't be the same storm front, but they appear to be on a collision course."

It was obvious Chad was going to get no sleep. He sat up and raised the seat back. "What happens then?"

"Don't think I've ever seen it," Dad said. "Don't think I want to either. We'll just speed it up here and plan on getting into Mukluk before either one of those fronts hits."

Though the heater in the ATV worked perfectly, icy drafts seeped in around Chad's window, making him hunker down in his down-filled parka.

"Cover the temperature without looking, Dad," he said. "Let's guess."

"Well, didn't we just hear it on the radio?"

"I didn't. But if you think you did, go ahead and guess."

"Low teens," Dad said, fingers covering the readout on the dash.

"Lower than that," Chad said. "Single digits."

Dad pulled his hand away. Five degrees. "What do you win?"

"I get to drive."

"Not a chance," Dad said smiling. "But let's guess how long it will take for the temperature to drop. I say we'll be down to zero within two hours."

"It's the middle of the day. I say it stays the same until late this afternoon."

"But we're heading toward two storms, Spitfire."

Chad shrugged. "So, if I'm wrong, you get to keep driving."

"Very funny."

Chad sat, shoulders hunched, drowsy in the blasts from the heater. It made him think of one of his and Kate's favorite phrases—"cotie, cotie"—their childhood way of saying "cozy." It had begun when their mother made a fire once when Dad was away. In their footie pajamas and blankets, they had settled in front of the fireplace with popcorn, singing, telling stories, and cuddling with Mom until Dad got home and joined them. Mom had said, "Isn't this cozy?"

And Kate had repeated, "Cotie."

Chad added, "Cotie, cotie."

And now "cotie, cotie" was how the whole family described such settings. When they were together and huddled against the cold, comfortable and warm and protected, the situation was "cotie, cotie."

But a glance at the horizon told Chad it wouldn't be that way in the ATV for long.

White on White

Chad stared. He'd never seen anything like it.

Dad got back on the radio. "This is Fighter Pilot in an ATV heading west, midway between Spike Mountain and Chandalar. Anybody coming east with a black cloud behind you?"

"Roger, ATV," came an immediate answer. "It's supposed to be just a snowstorm, but it looks like the thundershowers we used to get in Nebraska."

"Midwest boy, eh?" Dad said.

"Roger. You?"

"Michigan," Dad said.

"Close enough. This thing hasn't caught me yet, but I can see it. I'm trying to outrun it, hoping it turns one way or the other. You're going to run right into it. Where you headed?"

"Mukluk, over."

"A couple more hours if it stays dry."

"Dry as a bone right here," Dad said. "You may escape it altogether unless it runs you down."

"I'm keeping an eye on it in my rearview mirror, and I gotta tell you, it's coming fast. Black in the distance and cloudy above me already."

"You see clouds other than on the horizon?" Dad said. "I must be in a funny spot. Here it's just sun and blue skies, but dark on the horizon."

"You're in for a good show, Fighter."

"Wave at us when you pass," Dad said. "Red ATV."

"Roger, Fighter. I've got a big orange wrapper, heading for the railroads."

"How far out of Mukluk are you?" Dad said.

"About half an hour east," came the answer.

"Everything clear there?"

"It was. I gotta guess Mukluk is getting hit already."

"Should I dig in and hole up somewhere?"

"Where? There's precious little between where you are and Mukluk. I'd keep chugging. Still looks like just thunder clouds to me."

"Question is, is it the one out of Koyukuk or the one out of the Brooks Range?"

"Gotta be Koyukuk. Can't see anything out of the Brooks coming this low, can you?"

"Hope not."

"Good luck."

About forty-five minutes later Chad spotted the orange eighteen-wheeler in the distance. "There he is, Dad."

"Greetings from the Fighter, Orange Man," Dad said. "You copy?"

"Ten-four. I'm outrunning our dark chaser for now, but I understand it's hit Mukluk pretty heavy."

"Will I be able to get in there?" Dad said.

"Probably. I'm not seeing much traffic coming from your way. Other people scared to be out?"

"There's never much traffic up here, man," Dad said. "You ought to know that."

"I guess. But it's never this light except at night. Anybody ahead of me?"

"Come to think of it," Dad said, "we've passed only a couple of trucks and maybe three cars. You've got the road all to yourself."

"Don't know how good that is if the storm catches me."

"Take a big storm to stop you, Orange."

"Ten-four."

With that the big rig swept past them heading east. The driver waved and blew his huge air horns. Dad and Chad smiled and waved, and both drivers clicked their transmitters.

"This is fun," Chad said.

"For now," Dad said. "We don't want to get caught in a storm."

"If that rig can make it, we can."

"Oh, no. We're a whole lot lighter. We may be more maneuverable, but it takes a lot to stop a semi. We can pick our way through water and snow and ice, but if we get a whiteout, we're in trouble."

"Why? What happens?"

"It's impossible to see anything. Your headlights are useless. They just point directly into the swirling snow and shine right back into your eyes. And it doesn't make any difference whether it's day or night. The blizzard blinds you." He turned the heater down a notch. "During the day, the sun only makes everything whiter. At night, your headlights make it impossible. The only advantage at night is that you can sometimes see other headlights coming at you. But you never know if the other driver has seen you. All you can do is pull off the road as far as you can and keep your flashers on."

"Not your headlights?"

"They might be able to see your headlights better, but you risk blinding them too. If they don't see you till the last minute and you blind them with your lights, you're just as likely to get hit." Dad pressed his lips together, checked both side mirrors and the rearview mirror. "I'd turn back, but we're well over halfway home. And it might not be that bad. I've never seen a storm yet that I couldn't get through."

"I still say this is fun. It's kind of scary, but exciting. I wouldn't mind being caught in a blizzard again."

"You've never been in a real blizzard."

"Sure I have, Dad. I walked home through a huge snowstorm once."

"Did someone actually call it a blizzard?"

"Yeah."

"Well, a *real* blizzard is when there's so much snow that you can't see in front of your face. When you lose your orientation, have no idea which direction you're heading. We never would have let you walk home from school in a real blizzard."

"Don't you think it would be great though, Dad? To have to fight your way through the weather?"

"I thought so when I was a kid," Dad said. "Back then I thought everything turned out the way it was supposed to. TV shows and movies and books all seemed to have happy endings. But life's not like that, is it?"

Chad shook his head. He wasn't going to argue, but he still thought it would be fun to be stranded. Maybe not too far from home, but stranded anyway. How would they get out? What would they do?

His eyes felt heavy, so he closed them and thought about trekking through the frozen tundra. He woke sometime later with a start. It was cloudy and getting dark. "That came up awfully quick," he said.

"Not really," Dad said, driving more slowly. A freezing rain was hitting the windshield. "It's been building, and the road's slick. I just hope it dissipates as it heads east. It'd be nice if both those storms, whether they meet or not, would peter out before they hit Old Sparrow."

"How far are we from home?"

"About fifty miles."

The clock on the dash said three o'clock, and Chad went back to sleep. When he awoke in what seemed just a few minutes, Dad was hunched forward in the seat, his face even with the steering wheel.

"Whoa!" Chad said, peering into pitch blackness. "Welcome to Alaska. How long did I sleep anyway?"

"About an hour and a half."

"No kidding. How fast are you going? Or should I say how slow?"

"You tell me. I don't dare take my eyes off the road—or what I can see of it."

Chad studied the speedometer. “It’s hardly registering. How much farther to Mukluk?”

“Less than twenty miles,” Dad said. “But don’t get your hopes up. At this rate it might take us all night, if we get there at all.”

“We’ll get there,” Chad said. The temperature gauge read below zero. “How can it snow when it’s this cold?”

“I guess it’s just used to it.” Dad grinned but kept his eyes on the road. “Nobody ever told Alaska it was too cold for snow.”

A bright light suddenly flashed in the distance. “What was that?” Chad said.

“Lightning,” Dad said.

“Is that what Mr. Quenton was talking about?”

“Must be. Snow thunderstorms are supposed to be pretty common in the mountains. I’ve heard of them, but I’ve never been in one. They remind me of the tornadoes in the Midwest, so I don’t like them much.”

“I love them! I love storms! Especially when we’re safe and warm and together. Cotie, cotie.”

“Yeah, I hope,” Dad said. “I’d rather be cozy in our own house, wouldn’t you?”

“Yeah, but it wouldn’t be as exciting.”

"Driving like this is not exciting. The only two vehicles I've seen were heading the other way. A snowplow and a squad car, lights flashing."

"A snowplow going the other way?"

"Surprised me too, Spitfire. Go figure."

"We could sure use one going *this* way."

"I'd settle right in behind him," Dad said. He kept his eyes forward but rolled his head around, appearing to try to loosen his neck muscles. "Get on the CB and see who you can rouse."

"Are we too far from Old Sparrow to get the Quentons?"

"Oh, sure. Just ask for anybody traveling within fifty miles of Mukluk."

"Breaker, channel nineteen," Chad said, "this is Spitfire with Fighter Pilot, heading west into Mukluk. We going to make it?"

"Where are you, Spitfire?" came the reply.

"Twenty miles east," Chad said. "What's your handle?"

"ASPERN."

"ASPERN?" Chad repeated.

"Alaska State Police Emergency Radio Network. How many in your party?"

"Two," Chad said, "and it's no party."

"What're you driving?"

"Four-wheel ATV."

"Ten-four. Deep snow where you are?"

"Roger."

"You're going to have tough going, Spitfire. Consider pulling off and waiting this out. Emergency vehicles are busy in Mukluk. No electricity, power lines down, lots of accidents. If you're not hurt, try not to ask for help."

"Give me that," Dad said, taking the mike without looking.

"This is Fighter Pilot, ASPERN," he said. "Any advice on where we should go to wait this out?"

"If you're east, there's nothing till you get here. You live in Mukluk?"

"Roger."

"Better try to make it then. Got a generator at home?"

"Roger."

"You might want to get that going to keep your pipes from freezing."

"We're looking forward to relaxing by a warm fire, ASPERN."

"Roger. I know the feeling. I've been called to Venetie, and they don't even think it's the same storm."

"You're kidding! Is it the one that was supposed to have come out of the Brooks Range?"

"Roger. Don't know how it could have gotten past this front so fast and gone so far south. It's the bigger of the two, though. High winds, whiteouts, twisters, you name it."

"*Twisters*?"

"Well, not tornadoes, but close to it, they say. Better keep this frequency open, Fighter. Seventy-twos to you and Spitfire."

"Same back at ya," Dad said. "You'll be passing us here in a while if you're headed east. We're in a red ATV."

"Ten-four."

Half an hour later, as the ATV crawled along the covered roadway and Dad picked his way through the snow, trying to stay on course, Chad saw flashing police-car lights coming toward them. "That you, Fighter?" came the radio message.

"Ten-four."

"Deep drifts ahead of you. If you get hung up, are you prepared?"

"Ten-four."

"Need anything? I've got a few flares and some survival blankets."

"Got all we need, ASPERN."

"All the best."

Dad clicked his microphone twice, and they rolled slowly on into the storm.

Within minutes Dad had to downshift and weave across the road to stay in the shallowest drifts. Some were as deep as three feet already, and Chad tried to talk him into driving right through them, but Dad would have no part of it.

"Plowing through them might be fun at home, out of the storm, and on our own property," he said. "And we both know this rig can handle it. But we've got to get home. I hope this thing blows through and dies so we can get back to Old Sparrow by Tuesday."

"Storms around here never last long, do they?"

"Not usually, and it's a little early for one this severe. But sometimes they follow one right after another. That could strand us for days."

"Kate wouldn't mind. No school!"

"She'd have to go to school there, Chad. Those poor kids probably never get snowed out of school."

"Yuck."

"Let me show you what I mean about the headlights," Dad said and flashed the brights. They seemed to shine straight up. Chad squinted at the brilliant white light gleaming off the driving snowfall.

He nodded. "Wow."

Suddenly, no matter where Dad drove, the snow was two or three feet deep. Chad always loved to see his dad in action, doing whatever he had to do. He played with the controls, feathered the gas pedal, downshifted, steered this way and that, and kept driving. He was slipping and sliding, but the ATV was still upright and moving, though awfully slowly. Even with the oversized tires and the high ride, they could hear the snow scraping the bottom of the ATV.

"Hang on," he told Chad. "If we don't pick up some speed, we're going to get stuck in one of these drifts. Let me know if you see anything coming. I'm deciding right now to head right if we see anything coming at us."

Dad downshifted one more time and gunned the engine. The tires spun, then bit, and the car lurched. They probably weren't going more than twenty miles an hour, but after crawling along, to Chad it seemed they were flying. And for the first time he wondered what would happen if something appeared before them? Going this fast, would Dad be able to stop or swerve?

"If I can just get through this stretch and onto some clearer road," Dad said, "I think we can make it."

Dad ran smack into a five-foot drift, and the ATV nearly toppled, but he steered into the lean and they bounced and hit another drift. "Cool!" Chad shouted, but it wasn't as cool as all that. They couldn't go much farther unless they found shallower snow.

"Does it feel to you like we're still on the road?" Dad said.

"No clue!"

"I don't think we are," Dad said. "All I see is white. Just pray there are no ditches close by."

But there were. And Dad found a deep one.

On Foot

The ATV slipped off the steep shoulder, bouncing from one huge drift to another and then sliding backward into the ditch at the side of the road. Chad's head snapped back and his neck pressed hard against the headrest. He sat stunned as the headlights illuminated a tiny avalanche. Great chunks of snow slid over the hood of the car, covering the lights. In the eerie dimness, the light dancing in crazy directions as the lamps were covered, the last big wave of packed snow spread across the windshield.

Darkness engulfed them until Dad flipped on the inside lights. "You okay?" he said.

"Just whacked my head on the dash," Chad said, feeling a bump rising on his forehead.

Dad shifted into reverse and gunned the engine, then into drive and did the same. They were hung up, going nowhere. He shut off the engine.

"We'll freeze!" Chad shouted. "Turn that back on!"

"If I do, we'll be dead of carbon-monoxide poisoning. We've got to get out of here."

Dad unstrapped his seat belt and tried to open the door. It wouldn't budge. Chad pushed on his door. It opened about two inches. "I'm going to turn on the key just long enough so we can lower the windows," Dad said. "We'll have to dig out."

Dad pushed all four window buttons at once, and they whined down. Snow tumbled in around them. Something gave way above them with a thump, and Chad knew more snow was pressing on top of the car.

"There's not a lot of air left," Dad said. "Don't panic. Breathe normally and steadily, but start digging out. We don't know which way is softer or more shallow, so you go out your window and I'll go out mine."

"Where do we put the snow?" Chad said.

"Right behind us inside the car."

Dad crouched in the driver's seat and pulled on his huge mittens. He turned toward the open window and the snow pushing in around him and began pawing at it like a dog, sending it flying behind him onto the seat.

"Dad! Don't we need our stuff out of the back?"

"We'll come back for it! We need to tunnel out of here first."

Chad put on his gloves and hat and zipped his parka all the way to his neck. He copied his dad's position and started scooping snow behind him. Dad seemed to be getting nowhere but it wasn't long before Chad was able to crawl out and begin tunneling toward the surface, wherever that was.

He turned and hollered, "Dad, this way's easier! Follow me!"

Dad scrambled out through Chad's window and pressed up behind him. But the snow around the car was deep and soft. "Stand on my shoulders," Dad said, "and dig through to the top."

Chad grew panicky. Was he short of air? He was breathing heavily, but maybe it was just the work. Surely this was not like a real avalanche where the snow packs so tight and heavy that you might as well be encased in cement.

Chad struggled to step onto his dad's knees as Dad leaned back. A faint pinging noise in the car told him he hadn't shut his door after opening it a crack. The dim interior light was all he could see. He was fast growing claustrophobic and dug frantically, making the snow shift and fall all around Dad.

Strangely, it was cold, but not bitter; the avalanche protected them from the howling winds. When Chad reached the surface, he would be in the snowstorm, huge flakes blowing every which way and the wind stinging and freezing his exposed flesh. He wondered how far they were from home.

Chad set one foot on Dad's hip and reached higher, digging through the loosely packed snow and making it fall on his head, into his face, and down his body onto his father. "Sorry, Dad."

"Just keep going!" Dad shouted, as he grabbed Chad's boots and pushed. Chad was amazed at his dad's strength; it was as if he stood on a strong ladder, his dad pushing him higher as he scooped and scooped, trying to break through.

Finally Chad realized he was standing straight up, his dad with a hand under each boot, arms fully extended. He felt Dad's arms shaking; he surely couldn't hold Chad for long. Chad felt his own arms weakening as the blood rushed away from them. He pawed and scratched and dug with all his might.

Then, with one hand he broke through the snow. "I'm through!" he cried.

"Can you crawl out?" Dad said.

Chad stood on his tiptoes and reached with both hands, trying to gain purchase on the soft, shifting surface of the snow. He grabbed and pulled himself away from his dad, but as soon as he put all his weight on the snow, it crumbled beneath him. He seemed to be swimming, trying to stay above the drifts without pushing too much more down onto Dad.

"Dad! Are you all right?"

"I'm coming!" Dad shouted.

Chad barely heard the muffled sound. He decided to try to find some footing atop the snow and crab-walk away from the hole. Unfortunately, he had pushed chunks of snow behind him and into Dad's way.

"Just keep going!" Dad yelled. "I'll find you!"

Chad stretched out on the surface, trying to distribute his weight as evenly as possible so he wouldn't plunge back through. He wriggled and half crawled to where he thought the ATV was buried. He hoped it would provide a more solid base. The wind and snow bit into his face and his eyes stung. He brushed the snow away with his glove, but just smeared his vision more. Still, he thought he could make out the faint glow of the headlights under the snow.

Chad thought he heard Dad scratching his way to the surface behind him, but the wind was so strong and the snow so thick that he was afraid it was his imagination. He didn't know whether to move back to help Dad or stay where he was and let Dad find him.

"Dad!" he shouted.

"Stay where you are!" he heard faintly.

But Chad felt himself sliding, drifting with the shifting snow. He struggled to stay over the buried car, and when he felt his feet dropping, he windmilled with his hands, trying to stay upright. His boots finally stopped at something solid, and he realized he was standing tiptoe atop the ATV. The snow was up to just under his shoulders. Though encased in the snow bank, the lower part of his body felt warmer than the upper, which was exposed to the wind and watery snow. He oriented himself by the power-line poles, faced the road, and waited for his dad.

Soon a mittened hand thrust up out of the snow about six feet to his right, and Chad tried to reach it. He couldn't move. "Dad!" he shouted. "Over here!"

Dad thrashed and fought his way to the surface, then crab-walked until he slipped down into the snow and stood atop the ATV. Being a head taller than Chad, Dad stuck farther out of the snow.

"Now what?" Chad shouted above the violence of the storm.

"Now we breathe awhile," Dad said.

"How are we going to get home, Dad?"

"We'll need backpacks with some food. Flashlights. Snowshoes. Compasses."

"That's all in the car."

"I know. We'll have to dig down and get it, or we'll be stuck here. I'll make the first attempt."

"And what happens if the snow caves in on you?"

"Then you'll have to come and get me."

A few minutes later, Dad said, "Stay here."

"Like I've got a choice," Chad said, waving to show that only his arms would move.

Dad tunneled toward the passenger-side window and was soon out of sight. "Can you hear me?" he shouted.

"Yes!"

"I'm trying to keep an open area above me so I can breathe and come back the same way. I'll start tossing stuff to you. Be watching for it."

Chad thought he heard an engine in the distance, maybe a truck or car heading their way. He tried to clear his eyes and scan the horizon, but he saw nothing. He just felt the vibration and heard something.

"Dad! Can you hear that?"

No reply. Suddenly Chad heard the ATV start up. "Dad! What are you doing?"

Soon Dad returned to the surface, pushing two pairs of snowshoes and ski poles ahead of him. "Grab these!" he said.

"Why'd you start the car?" Chad said.

"It might melt some snow and be easier to pull out later. I have to keep an eye on it though, because if there's snow packed in the exhaust pipe, it'll cause a backup, overheat, and maybe catch fire."

Dad went back down. The wind shifted and calmed, and Chad thought he detected two headlights far in the distance to the west. Before he could say anything, Dad tossed him two backpacks and shouted, "We're overheating! I've got to turn it off!"

"But Dad!" Chad said too late. Dad had disappeared.

The truck sound grew louder, and a snowplow came into view. It was moving more slowly than Chad had ever seen one go. The drifts before it were so huge that it couldn't just blast through as usual. This plow would get up some speed, then seem to waver and even wobble, then slow and start again.

Finally, about a quarter mile from where Chad stood anchored in the snow, the snowplow began to pick up speed. Soon it was noisily humming along, pushing four- and five-foot drifts ahead of it and off to the side. There was only one problem—it was on the wrong side of the road!

The driver couldn't possibly see Chad—the snow was so deep. But the plow was in the westbound lane, heading east and pushing snow off to its left. Chad stood right in the path of the hurtling snow.

Chad waved and shouted and then screamed as the snowplow bore down on him. He knew the plow blade wouldn't hit him, because if the truck got that close to the edge of the road, it would tumble down into the ditch with the ATV.

The driver wasn't slowing. Chad wished he had a flashlight. "Dad!" he shouted, and then the plow came roaring by going at least forty miles an hour. He hid his face with his arms, and rocks and dirt and snow blasted him. The plow dumped hundreds of pounds of snow in the ditch, covering him. He had no idea how deep the snow was above him now.

"What was that?" Dad shouted, sounding far away.

"Snowplow!" Chad hollered.

"You all right?"

"Buried!" Chad said.

"Dig yourself out again, Spitfire. You're not under big drifts now. I've got everything, and I'm coming up!"

Chad huffed and puffed as he dug and scrambled up. Scraping through the freshly plowed snow and dirt and rocks was the hardest part of the ordeal so far. But, finally, he reached the howling wind and gulped the frigid, but precious, air. He crawled nearer the road, up out of the ditch to where he could stand on the plowed road. He turned to wait and watch for Dad.

When Dad's head finally popped up out of the snow, Chad waved.

"Where are the rest of our supplies?" Dad yelled.

"Under the snow somewhere!"

"We've got to have them, Spitfire! Help me dig."

Chad was so exhausted by the time they had spread-eagled their bodies and picked through the snow for their supplies that he could hardly get up. "We don't need the snowshoes, do we," he said, "now that the road is plowed?"

"We don't know how far it's plowed or how long it'll be clear," Dad said. "We'd better take them anyway. We have to keep moving. Just be glad you don't live near the South Pole."

"Why?" Chad said. They were on solid ground now, strapping on their backpacks, checking their flashlights, and tying their snowshoes around their shoulders.

"The South Pole hovers around one hundred degrees below zero during the winter, especially during the months when the sun doesn't shine. Then in the summer, the temperature shoots as high as sixty or even thirty degrees *below*. They think it's balmy."

Somehow, talking about a place even more frigid and miserable than where he was didn't make Chad feel any warmer. "How far do you figure we'll have to walk?" he said.

"We're less than ten miles from home," Dad said, "but I sure hope we'll see someone on the road before we have to walk that far. Let's each eat a granola bar or some trail mix. We're going to need the energy."

They trudged off into the darkness, eating and leaning into the wind. At one point Dad stopped and dug out some petroleum jelly, which he smeared on both their faces. Snow was drifting across the road again, and they soon had to stop and put on their snowshoes. Chad had always compared walking in snowshoes to walking with tennis rackets tied to your boots. They took some getting used to, but it was a lot easier going than sliding a foot or two into the snow with every step.

Two hours later Chad didn't feel as if they had gone far at all. They were wet, cold, exhausted, and hungry again. Dad found two more granola bars in Chad's backpack, and they ate them quickly.

"Can we make it all the way?" Chad said.

"We have to, Spitfire. There's no shelter anywhere but back at the car, and if we cleared the snow around it, it could get buried again. We just have to put one foot in front of the other until we get home. Just through those trees over there you can see the lights of Mukluk."

It sure looked far away. But just then all the lights in Mukluk went out.

"They'll come back on," Dad said. "Remember the trooper told us the power was off hours ago. It came back on then. It'll come back on again."

"I'm glad you're so sure," Chad muttered. "Because I'm not."

"Keep trudging, big guy," Dad said. "Sometimes tough times get easier when you're down to fewer options. Right now we have only one. Keep going."

Home

Dad tried to motivate Chad as they marched through the blowing snow. "*Left*, right, *left*, right, *left*." He made up silly ditties to keep them moving. "*Left*, right *left*, right. I *left* my wife and thirty-one children at *home* in the kitchen without any gingerbread *left*. *Left*, right, *left*."

The petroleum jelly smeared on his otherwise exposed cheeks helped a little, but still Chad was cold to the bone. His feet felt like huge blocks of ice attached to the wide snowshoes, but he forced himself to keep lifting his knees and trudging along. Dad stopped occasionally to shine his flashlight on the compass.

"If I have it figured right, we're on a direct course to our house."

Chad saw no cars, no trucks, no snowplows, no lights, no moon, no stars, no anything. Suddenly Dad turned off the highway and started through a wide-open plain toward a forest in the distance.

"Shouldn't we stay near the road, just in case?" Chad said.

"We might as well walk in a straight line toward home, rather than on the road. You want to sing?"

"Dad, the last thing I want to do is sing."

"You want me to sing?"

"Check that. The second to the last thing I want to do is sing. The very last thing I want to do is hear you sing."

Dad laughed. "I wonder how far the storm extends."

"This one or the one out of the Brooks Range?" Chad said.

"Either. I just wonder if the snow has hit Old Sparrow yet."

For several hours—Chad guessed three or four—they trudged on. Dad flashed his light between trees to areas they could walk, calling out frequently to encourage Chad or stopping for water. The woods seemed to protect the ground from the bigger drifts, and while they were still probably two feet above the soil, at least they weren't slogging through the really deep snow.

Finally, as they came into a clearing, they looked up and the storm had blown over. No more snow. No more cloud cover. The wind was even slowing. Chad was struck by the beauty of the early-morning sky. It was a velvety blue-black. The stars were still ablaze.

"We should be home within the hour," Dad said. "It'll still be dark, but we'll get there."

Chad picked up his pace with that news. He and Dad ate the rest of the trail mix and granola bars, and he felt a brief surge of energy. Sometimes he shut his eyes and pretended he was sleepwalking. He no longer had to fight the wind and the watery flakes, so he could breathe easier, but he still didn't know how he could keep going for another hour. He was numb. Every muscle ached. Like a toddler in a snowsuit, he walked stiff-legged, carefully lifting his feet enough to make the snowshoes work the way they were designed.

Dad wrapped an arm around Chad's shoulders. "When we get home, we'll make a big fire in the fireplace and I'll get the gas generator going. We'll see if the phones are working, and I'll try to call Old Sparrow. We'll change our clothes and sleep in front of the fire under the biggest quilts we have."

"I wish I could sleep now!" Chad muttered.

"Me too, Spitfire," Dad said. "Me too."

Nearly an hour later, Dad said, "Chad, would you like to see the prettiest sight I've seen in a long time? Look straight ahead."

Dad shined his powerful flashlight beam into the distance, and Chad could barely see the outline of the small hangar at the edge of their property where Dad kept two of his remaining double-engine planes. “Thank God,” Chad said. It still looked a long way off.

“Come on,” Dad said. “Just stay steady, and we’ll get there.”

When they finally got to the fence outside the hangar, Dad held the barbed wire down so Chad could flop over. One of his snowshoes got hung up, and he fell face first into the snow. He quickly brushed himself off, thinking how predictable that had been. As if they hadn’t already been through enough.

Dad paused. “I don’t even want to think about how frozen those engines are in the unheated hangar.”

Chad walked on alone, his eyes on the garage and then the back door of the house.

“The hangar doors are frozen shut and drifted over,” Dad said, catching up.

Chad couldn’t even grunt. All he wanted was to get inside.

The garage was also entombed in snow, and when they reached the back door of the house, they had to dig several feet of snow away before it would open. Chad staggered up the steps. Everything was dark, and the house was cold, but it was warmer than being outside.

“Get out of those clothes and get dried off,” Dad said, starting to peel off his own stuff. “Massage your fingers and toes to get the blood circulating. I'm going to get the generator going."

A few moments later, wood was piled high in the fireplace, and the radio was tuned to the emergency weather station. Chad laid quilts out in front of the fireplace while his dad lit the fire. When the lights came on, Dad started heating cider in the electric coffee pot.

"Phone lines are dead," Dad said. "Bring your laptop down."

"What if my battery's low?"

"I have another socket on the generator."

Chad shuddered. "Let me get warm first."

"Fair enough. I don't suppose there's anything we can do for anybody right now anyway, no matter what they need."

Chad curled up in a sleeping bag under a quilt. He watched as Dad unplugged the answering machine from the wall. He plugged it into the generator, which was vented to the outside so the exhaust wouldn't create carbon monoxide in the house.

The generator was so loud that Chad couldn't hear the clicking of the machine as it reset itself and Dad played back the messages. "Chad!" he said. "Come and listen."

Chad was finally warm and comfortable and almost asleep, but he crawled out from under the covers and leaned in toward the answering machine. The message was from the Old Sparrow Christian School.

"Bruce, this is Hugh Quenton. It's pitch black here, and it's the middle of the afternoon. The forecasts are scary. Thunder snowstorms are coming from two directions and are expected to converge. They're predicting twister-type winds, several inches of snow, closed roads, and probably power and phone outages. Your daughter is at the computer now, trying to bang out a message to you so you'll get it before we lose power."

Chad would have to check his email right away.

"We've got a problem here, buddy, some kind of an epidemic. A lot of our kids and staff have come down with it, and we don't know what it is. Kate and Sue both show symptoms. I'm not feeling so hot myself, and though Marge won't admit it, I think she's coming down with it too."

Dad frowned. "Oh, Katie," he whispered.

"Seems like anybody who had any contact with the infirmary or with people who were in the infirmary are getting it and getting it quick," Mr. Quenton said. "We've got a call in to the druggist in Old Sparrow, but he says the last he heard his air shipment made it as far as McDougall Pass. That's about a hundred miles to the east of him. By the time he gets the stuff, if he does, it's unlikely we'll be able to get to him or him to us."

"Dad! We can get it!"

"*Shhh!*"

"We need antibiotics, and we need them in a bad way. And Sue needs more of her insulin sometime within the next two days." Mr. Quenton paused, and Chad heard a dim rumbling. "Did you hear that? That's thunder! Never heard thunder in the winter before." Heavy static crackled on the line. "It's starting to rain here, Bruce, of all things. Looks like a heavy sleet on the windows, and like I say, it's dark as night here."

Chad didn't like the sound of Mr. Quenton's voice.

"I'd better get off the phone, but if you could call someone, let authorities know, get us some help or something, I'd sure appreciate it. Hope you and Chad get home all right and that your place is spared whatever's coming at us. Call us if you can and—"

Mr. Quenton was cut off by a huge boom, more static, and then nothing. The next message was from the Mukluk Sheriff, asking Dad if he could help with emergency relief in town. "We don't expect to have power much longer, Bruce, but call us if you can."

"I can't call anybody," Dad said, checking the phone again. "I can't believe Katie's sick already. I wish she were with us." He paused. "Come on, let's pray."

After praying for everyone sick at the school, Dad ran an extension cord from the generator to the radio and set the radio near the fireplace, far enough from the generator that they could hear it.

"I'd like to get word to the state police about our car," Dad said. "And I'd like to offer to help with the relief effort in town."

"Get some sleep," Chad managed. "You can't help anybody now."

"You're probably right." Dad collapsed into his bedroll and was asleep before Chad. Chad fell asleep listening to local weather reports and emergency bulletins that merely told him what he had walked through.

Chad slept so soundly that when he awoke several hours later he was in the exact position as when he'd gone to sleep. He dragged himself out of his sleeping bag and stoked the fire, adding logs until it burst back to life. Dad stirred, rolled over, and kept sleeping. Chad sat near the fire, still tired and achy, but feeling a lot better. It was snowing, not heavily, but enough to cover the drifts with a fresh blanket.

Chad checked the phone. Still dead. He went to his cold room, grabbed his laptop, set it next to the generator and booted up. He found several email messages, mostly junk except for Kate's. He'd never seen her so urgent.

"We all have fevers," she wrote, "and huge storms are coming. If I wasn't sick and if I couldn't tell from the others how much sicker I'm going to be, I'd love being stranded here with Suzie Q. She only has a little medicine left, and her parents feel guilty about that. But they did all they could. They arranged for more to be flown in, in plenty of time, but who knew the storms would come? We're supposed to lose power too. I feel so achy and sick. I hope they get some medicine in here soon. When you come back, call me on your wrist TV when you're within a mile or so. Write back as soon as you get this."

Chad quickly answered, wondering if Kate would be well enough to read it. He went back to the fireplace and listened to the radio, keeping the volume low to let his dad sleep. What he heard gave him chills all over again.

"This is the last report from the United States Weather Bureau headquartered in Beaver in the Yukon Flats. Even by northern Alaskan standards, the twin thunder snowstorms that have ravaged the northeastern part of the state have been record breaking. A huge front rolling out of the Brooks Range north of the Kobuk Valley has caught, overtaken, and mixed with the same sort of storm front that seems to have originated in the Bering Strait, swept through Kotzebue Sound, gained momentum in Koyukuk, and blasted through Mukluk yesterday.

"These twin storm fronts, either of which alone has the potential for mass destruction, now form one giant weather pattern that has hugged the frozen Porcupine River bed. The new hybrid storm picked up steam, rolling over Spike Mountain near the Canadian border, dumping several inches of hail, ice, rain, and snow on the area in a direct line with McDougall Pass.

"Old Sparrow and everything to the west is under heavy drifts, and the snow continues with high winds, downed power and phone lines, impassable roads, and communications virtually at a standstill. Except for infrequent shortwave radio traffic, no news is going into or coming out of the region."

Chad leaned closer to the radio.

"Ironically," the newscaster continued, "yet another huge blizzard has settled in McDougall Pass and threatens to join the others to form a three-headed monster, the likes of which even this area has never seen. One can only imagine the destruction. Emergency medical technicians and power and phone company employees are working to bring relief to tiny Mukluk. Power is being returned slowly, though phone lines may be down for days."

Chad wished Dad had heard this. But on the other hand, he was glad Dad was still asleep. Dad had this thing about wanting to be in the center of the action, going where he was needed, doing whatever needed to be done. That was all well and good, but he needed his sleep—and it was still dangerous out there. Chad didn't know where and when they would be needed, but if his dad got his rest, he would be ready when the time came.

There would be plenty of work to go around, and Chad knew Dad would be eager to somehow get back to Old Sparrow. Those people, including Kate, were in deep trouble. If this bug and Suzie Q's diabetes could not be treated, they faced dangers worse than the snowstorms.

Venturing Out

In the morning Dad did wonders with the electric skillet. Although they had only bacon and eggs, Chad couldn't remember such a tasty and filling breakfast. After checking the dead phones again, Dad assigned Chad the task of packing everything they would need for a flight into the storm area.

"A *flight*?" Chad said.

Dad nodded. "We'll use the ski plane. There'll be no driving in there, maybe for days. We can't leave those people stranded. I may be the only one who can get into town if those medicines do arrive. And if they don't, I may have to meet the delivery pilot in McDougall Pass."

Chad slowly shook his head.

"You don't have to come along if you don't want to," Dad said. "But I could use you on the radio while I'm keeping an eye on the weather and the ground."

"Of course I want to come. I can just hardly believe you're doing this."

"Chad, my only daughter is in there with a family I've cared about for years, not to mention all those kids I don't even know. If I were a parent of one of them, I would want to believe somebody was making an effort to get in there with help."

"But aren't the authorities doing that? They have to know that the school is stranded."

"I'm sure they do, Chad, but what can they do? You know every law enforcement and emergency team is overloaded just trying to restore power and make the roads passable."

Chad packed food, first-aid stuff, extra clothes, gloves, boots, and hats. He also gathered their snowshoes and snowmobile suits. And, as Kate suggested, he included their wrist TVs.

Meanwhile Dad rigged up his gasoline feeder to allow a supply of fuel to run continually to the generator. It had an automatic shutoff when electrical power to the house kicked back on.

"How long can it run?" Chad said.

"Nonstop for forty-eight hours. We'll run some electric heaters to keep the water pipes from freezing."

As Chad tied the bundles he would load onto the ski plane (the one with landing skis as well as retractable wheels), he saw Dad shoveling snow from in front of the hangar. He jogged out to help. The snow had diminished to just flurries, but it was bitterly cold.

"Finish this patch here so we can roll the plane out," Dad said, "and I'll see if I can get this door open."

Chad knew the hangar door to be stubborn even in the best of weather. It was a huge, corrugated steel thing that ran on wheels and slid across the opening. It was old, heavy, creaky, and ornery, and now it was frozen in place.

Dad yanked on it, kicked it, then rammed it with his shoulder. Chad ran over and added his own shoulder. When it seemed to break free a bit, Dad shook it and tried to drag it open, but it wouldn't budge. He went through a side door and began banging on the big door from the inside. Soon he came back outside carrying one of the pressurized tanks filled with deicer that was usually used on the wings. He sprayed it all over the door.

When it finally opened, Dad slipped inside the frigid Quonset hut and slid the door shut again.

"What are you doing?" Chad said.

"We've got a lot of work to do on the plane before we can back it out of here," Dad said. "We don't need that cold wind."

"Why didn't we work on the plane before we opened the door?"

"For the same reason we're not going to load the plane until we make sure the engines work. What if we couldn't open the door after getting the plane ready? We would have wasted our effort."

Dad sprayed deicer directly onto the engine and began tinkering with all the various parts—spark plugs, coils, propellers, everything. "It's going to work," he said finally. "You can start loading up."

"And can I open the big door?"

"You may."

After Chad's third trip from the house with the supplies, he was shivering and his face stung. It reminded him of their all-night walk, and he really wanted to forget about that. Dad had jumped inside the tiny cockpit and tried to fire up the engines, but only the right one came to life. He shut it off, then stuck his head out and motioned to Chad.

"Hand crank the left prop and then get back!"

Chad turned the left propeller with both hands the way he had watched his dad do it many times. When he felt it tighten and ready to spring, he jumped out of the way and Dad flipped the switch. Soon both engines roared and began that high-pitched hum. The wind gusts caused by the powerful blades blasted against the sides of the hangar and threatened to push Chad outside.

Dad signaled that Chad should step aside and shut the door after the plane was outside. As the noisy thing passed him, Chad pressed his back up against the wall. Once outside on the packed snow, Dad retracted the wheels. He settled the plane down on its landing skis and waited until Chad had rolled the big door shut, locked it, and climbed aboard.

Dad taxied into a clearing near the house and sat, letting the engines whir as he radioed into town. He reached the Alaska State Police Emergency Radio Network and found the chaos he'd expected. Everyone had been working twenty-four hours, he was told. Dad informed them of the approximate location of the ATV, adding, "I don't expect to see it soon, but I want you to know it's buried out there so we don't lose it forever."

"No promises," he was told. "But thanks. We'll watch for it and let you know."

Then Dad filed his flight plan with the local airport control tower. "You're going where, over?" he was asked.

"Trying to get as close to Old Sparrow as possible."

"You know about the weather there?"

"Fully informed," Dad said. "They have medical emergencies, and no one else is getting in or out."

"And you're going to do it with a ski plane?"

"No choice."

"We can't forbid you, but the odds are against you."

"I'll be careful. I should be able to put down anywhere."

"But you realize what could happen if—"

"Totally cognizant," Dad said, and Chad could tell he was getting frustrated. "The longer I talk to you, the worse the weather gets over there."

Chad wasn't confident about getting off the unevenly snow-packed ground. With wheels on dry ground, it was easy. But sliding along on skis over packed and drifted snow—he wasn't so sure.

As was his custom, Dad prayed before they took off. He asked for guidance and safety and for God to make a way where none seemed to exist.

Dad cranked the throttle up full, and the little craft seemed to sit on its haunches, just waiting to break free. Rattling and vibrating at full tilt, the little plane seemed to paw at the ground and flit around in the wind. Dad maneuvered the controls quickly so they began their takeoff at top speed. Chad sat there, tightly buckled in, gripping the sides of his chair, his eyes fixed on the snow-covered ground.

The craft cut through the tops of high, powdery drifts, then dipped to bounce off deep, more tightly packed snow. Chad knew there was no turning back. There were no brakes with the skis down, so even if Dad had aborted right then, they would have slid wildly to a stop. With snow like this, who knew what would happen if he dropped the wheels so that they could dig into the snow and come to a halt? Dad was playing the controls like a big musical instrument, and Chad knew the flaps were dancing, trying to direct the air stream and push their overgrown hummingbird into the air.

Chad felt the plane rise only a bit, then a little more. Finally, they swept into the air, the fuselage shuddering and the little plane breaking free of gravity. Chad had been holding his breath, and now he let out a huge sigh. "Thank You, Lord," he said aloud.

Dad smiled. "Never a doubt," he said.

"Maybe not in your mind," Chad said.

Dad laughed.

Chad studied the ground. "It took us all night to walk nearly ten miles in the snow after driving several hours. How long a flight is this?"

"We'll be able to go as the crow flies, in other words, in a straight line. We don't have to follow the highway, which was built to follow the curves of the river. So if we fly all the way to the city of Old Sparrow, I'm guessing it's about 250 miles. Not a long flight."

"Are you going to fly all the way to Old Sparrow?"

"We'll see after we talk to the Quentons, provided I can rouse them on the radio. I have to know the medical situation and if they know whether the medicine has arrived in the city. If the medicine has no way of getting to the school and the school has no way of getting to it, then yes, we'll try to put down near the city so we can pick it up."

The first hour and a half of the flight was uneventful. Chad peered down on the river, the highway, and the tiny villages, and nothing seemed to be moving. It was as if northeast Alaska had been turned into a ghost town, but rather than dust and dirt covering everything as it did in Old West ghost towns, mounds of snow lay over the frozen cars, trucks, buildings, and ground. Here and there a plume of smoke from a vent atop a house puffed out the news that someone was trying to keep warm. The occasional snowplow worked slowly with front-end loaders, clearing small sections of highway at a time.

"I don't like what I'm seeing on the horizon." Dad glanced at his watch. "Almost three, and look at that sky."

Although daylight was nearly gone, the horizon looked particularly dark and ominous. "How far from the school are we?" Chad said.

"Should be reachable by radio. See if you can raise them."

Dad had assigned to the ski plane the call letters of the plane destroyed in Indonesia the previous summer. Chad announced, "November, November double Hotel forty forty-eight to ground at Old Sparrow Christian School. Do you read? Over."

Chad and Dad heard nothing but static. Chad repeated the call. Still nothing.

"Change frequencies," Dad suggested. "Just stay off the emergency band, because the local authorities will be all over that."

Chad tried a couple of other channels. Finally he heard the voice of a young man "Hello? Hello? Are you calling us?" the man said, his voice cracking.

"Calling Old Sparrow Christian School," Chad said.

"That's us!" he said. "I'm supposed to be manning the radio, but I don't really know what I'm doing. This is the first call I've got. Who is this, and what do you want?"

"My name is Chad. My dad and I are on an airplane coming at you from the west. We're friends of the Quentons. What's your name?"

"Mike."

"Listen, Mike, we need to talk to Mr. or Mrs. Quenton."

"They're real sick, just like most everybody here. I don't feel so good myself, but there are about twenty or so of us who aren't sick. We're waiting for medicine from Old Sparrow."

Dad took the microphone. "Mike, this is Chad's dad. I'm the pilot. Where's everybody staying?"

"In their rooms and in classrooms. There's only room for about twelve in the infirmary. They started putting people in classrooms, but they ran out of cots. They were trying to keep the infected people from exposing the others, but they finally had to let people just go to their own beds. I guess we've all been exposed to this by now."

"What is it? Do you know?"

"Mrs. Quenton said it's called strep-something. Anyway, it's highly contagious and strong."

"Does she think it's deadly?" All he could think of was Kate. "Do you know anything about my daughter, Kate? She's staying with the Quentons."

"Sorry, no, I don't. Mrs. Quenton doesn't think the virus is deadly, but she's worried about what might happen to people who carry high fevers too long. We need antibiotics from Old Sparrow."

"Any word on whether they have a supply?"

"Yes! We heard from the drugstore there that they met the flight somewhere near McDougall Pass and got back as far as Old Sparrow, but they can't come any farther. The roads are closed and snowed and drifted over, and there's no power in Old Sparrow now either."

"How did you get power?"

"Mr. Quenton hooked the radio and some heaters up to a generator, but we're low on gas. He's only running it every other half hour."

"How's he doing?"

"Not good. He just tells us what to do from his bed. He's got the fever and chills like everybody else."

"How's the food supply?"

"We put the frozen stuff outside, and there seems to be enough for a while. The sick people aren't hungry, and the well people are scared. It's still snowing and blowing here. That storm last night and this morning was unbelievable."

"You know you got two of them at the same time."

"Three, actually. We got the McDougall Pass front too."

"Wow."

"It was awful. We thought the roof was going to blow off the main building. The Quentons' house lost most of its windows and part of its roof. Nobody can be in there now."

Chad grabbed the mike. "How's Suzie Q?"

"Who?"

"Sue Quenton!"

"Not good. She's real low on her medicine. She's got some other kind of a disease, you know, and they've cut her doses in half, but I guess it's not working. The drugstore in Old Sparrow has what she needs too, but we've got to have it fast."

"We're over you right now," Dad told Mike. "We're going to try to put down in Old Sparrow, get Sue's insulin, and bring it back to you. What else do you need?"

"Gas!" he shouted. "We're low. We've been running the generator on gas from the cars. They can't go anywhere anyway."

"Tell the Quentons we're on our way!"

But when Chad and Dad came within visual range of Old Sparrow, Chad could hardly believe his eyes. The town appeared to have been destroyed by a tornado. He'd heard that twister-type winds were part of at least two of the three storms that had converged on the little town, but he hadn't expected to see houses in pieces and roofs torn off several structures.

Worse, from what Chad could see, there was nowhere to land their plane and be certain that it wouldn't hit debris under the snow.

Plan B

"You've heard of Plan A and Plan B?" Dad said.

"Yeah," Chad said. "But I guess I never knew what it meant."

"Well, Plan A is your original plan — the easiest, most logical solution to a problem. Our plan was to fly to Old Sparrow, get the medicine, fly to the school and deliver it, and see what we could do about helping those people."

"And bring Kate home."

"Of course. As soon as she's able to fly. But look what happened to Plan A."

Chad looked down at Old Sparrow again as Dad circled. "Snow happened to Plan A," Chad said.

"Worse than snow," Dad said. "That was some kind of major storm, maybe three at once."

Chad nodded. "So what's Plan B?"

"We've got to find a place to put down and then walk into Old Sparrow to get that medicine. Suzie Q's life is in danger, and who knows how sick Katie is? And all those adults and other kids who need antibiotics — who knows what might happen to them? This thing may not be fatal, but how can we know what damage it's doing to their systems?"

"But Dad, look," Chad said, pointing. The ground was covered with huge drifts for miles in every direction surrounding Old Sparrow. "If we find a place to land, it will take us hours to get into and out of Old Sparrow. And how do we know if anyone is still alive down there or if the drugstore is open or even if we can get through the drifts on foot? We should have brought snowmobiles."

"Shoulda, woulda, coulda never gets you anywhere," Dad said. "We couldn't fit a snowmobile in this plane, and it would have been too heavy anyway. We'll just have to scout out a place to put down as close as possible and take our chances. That's Plan B. There are no alternatives. Meanwhile, see if you can raise anybody on the radio in Old Sparrow."

Chad tried every channel, getting no response.

"They may be on batteries only," Dad said, "and on the air only a few minutes every hour. Keep trying. And try the emergency channel if all else fails."

Dad was now flying back toward the Old Sparrow Christian School, thirty miles west of the town of Old Sparrow. The plane circled in wider and wider arcs as Dad looked for open areas. Chad finally raised a medical technician on the emergency channel.

"Roger, I read you November, November double Hotel," he said. "Unless your call is urgent, we need to keep this channel clear."

Chad told him the situation.

"Nothing's getting in or out of that area for at least twenty-four hours," the emergency medical technician said. "And we're warning small aircraft to stay out of there too. More weather is coming from the pass soon."

"McDougall?"

"Roger. Something's building in there again."

"That's all we need."

"Roger," the EMT said. "Wish we could help, but the snowplows are moving mighty slow. We've had limited radio contact with Old Sparrow, but their power is down. They're on batteries the first ten minutes of every hour. Several deaths there, lots of injuries. They're our top priority, but we appreciate knowing about the school too. Nothing we can do there for at least twenty-four hours." He signed off.

"Chad, look," Dad said as he circled a wide open field. "That looks pretty smooth. I don't detect anything beneath the surface."

Chad studied it. "Sure seems a long way from Old Sparrow. I can't even see the town from here."

"If you look back this way you can," Dad said. "About twenty miles."

"We're going to walk *twenty* miles into town, and *twenty* back to the plane?"

"We're going to do what we have to do, son."

"Won't it be dark by then?"

"We've got flashlights."

"Wait. We're closer to the Christian school than to the town, right?"

"Oh, yeah."

"Then why don't we put down closer to the school and see if we can get that old snow remover of theirs working?"

Dad frowned. "It's a long shot."

"It's worth a try. It would take us the whole day to walk twenty miles each way through this stuff, especially after last night. And with another storm coming? And who can say we would even be able to get past all the drifts?"

Dad rubbed his forehead. "You're right, " he said. "Try to get Mike back on the radio. We need to find out if they've siphoned the fuel out of the snow remover."

Chad got no response. Then suddenly the radio crackled to life. "November, November, double Hotel forty forty-eight airborne, do you read? This is Old Sparrow, over."

"Go ahead, Old Sparrow."

"We're on just a few minutes an hour here—down to batteries—but we got word from an EMT that you were trying to reach us."

"Yeah." Chad quickly ran down the situation at the Christian school and what they planned.

"I'll get in touch with the pharmacist and see what he's got, November Hotel. No one's heard from him since he got back from McDougall with the stuff, just before the twisters hit."

"You think he's all right?"

"Couldn't tell you. The store seems all right, but of course it's not open. Nothing's happening here. Relief is on its way from state and federal agencies, they tell us, but we've got a mess."

"Ten-four. We'll probably see you later today to try to get some of that medicine."

"I don't know how you'll ever get in here, but good luck."

They were soon within sight of the Christian school. It looked as lifeless as Old Sparrow but without as much destruction. A long smooth stretch of snow lay on both sides of the main buildings. Dad buzzed the complex, and

Chad heard a staticky transmission on his wrist TV. He pulled his sleeve back and tuned it in. "Kate?" he said. "Are you there?"

"I'm here, Chad," came his sister's hoarse voice. The LCD picture was fuzzy. "What are you guys doing up there? Do you have the medicine?"

"Kate!" Dad yelled over the engine noise. "Are you all right? You sound awfully weak."

"I'm okay, Dad, really," she said. "Or I will be."

Chad brought her up to date and told her their plan to try to get into Old Sparrow in the dilapidated snowplow.

"They say that thing has been used only a couple of times in the last few months," she said. "I don't even know if it would get that far. Mr. Quenton only uses it to plow the driveways and get the drifts away from the front of the buildings."

"Well, it's Plan B, but it's all we've got," Chad said. "Dad wants to know if there's gas in the snowplow."

"We'll let you know," Kate said.

"When will Mike be back on the radio?"

"The first half hour of every hour," she said. "But I can tell you over the wrist TVs."

"That's only if we're close enough," Chad said. "It's hard to hear. We'll be landing pretty soon, but we don't want to be exposed to anybody who's sick. Just have him tell us whether the thing is gassed up or where the gas supply is if it's not."

"We're low on gas, I know that," Kate said. "Because of the generator. We've got food—"

"Outside, yeah, I know," Chad said. "Mike told us. Have him call us on the radio at the top of the hour. That's just a few minutes from now."

"That's the snowplow right there, isn't it?" Dad pointed at a snow-covered contraption near one of the buildings.

The huge old truck had a plow on the front, double tires on each back axle, and a gigantic snowblower built onto one side. It was a dump truck, but the bed appeared empty except for snow.

"Looks like it," Chad said. "You think it'll get us anywhere in this snow?"

"It's our only hope," Dad said. "I just hope you're up to helping me shovel salt or gravel or dirt or something up into the back of that thing. If that truck bed is empty, we'll slide all over the roads and likely bounce right out of the cab. If we can fill it, it should drive through anything."

"How long will it take to fill it?"

"I don't want to think about it. I sure hope there are chains on the tires."

"There have to be, right?"

"Not necessarily. Those are big tires with deep treads, and if they only use it here on the complex, they might not have put chains on it. Those are probably old tires though, so if chains are available, I'll want them."

Dad made one more pass over the school complex.

"How are we doing on fuel?" Chad said.

"We're fine," Dad said. "We have plenty to get us back home if we don't go anywhere else."

"Sure wish we were flying to Old Sparrow."

"Me too. But wishing doesn't get us anywhere. The Lord has been with us so far, even last night. Just keep praying."

"I still can't believe we made it all the way home."

"I know, Chad. We could have easily been buried in the ATV or frozen to death on the road." Dad scanned the ground. "That looks good, right there."

The plane's descent felt too fast to Chad. "Should you slow down a little?" he said.

"Can't risk stalling. The engines would never refire in this weather. If you think it's cold out there, imagine the windchill we're generating at over a hundred miles an hour. I've got lots of room to slide once we touch down. I just hope it's all smooth and that there are no surprises under the snow."

The plane turned and dipped, then leveled off before starting to rapidly descend. It felt like they were diving straight down, and Chad's heart pounded just like when they'd crashed in Indonesia earlier in the year. He hung on and prayed.

Dad leveled off again, and all Chad could see was white. The ground was snow covered, of course, but even the sky, cloud covered in the middle of the afternoon, looked white to him. How could Dad keep his bearings, his perspective?

At the first touch of the skis to the snow, the plane bounced and swerved left. Dad straightened it in the air, and then they touched down again and began a long, fast slide. The plane glided smoothly along the snow, hardly seeming to slow.

"Perfect," Chad said.

"Not yet," Dad said. "What's that up there?"

Chad stared straight ahead. Something loomed in front of them now that hadn't been visible from the sky. The snow-covered mound had somehow blended in with the ground when looked at from above.

"I don't know!" Chad said. "Can you miss it?"

"Have to try," Dad said, playing with the flaps. With no brakes on landing skis, all he could do was try to turn, but at that speed, turning could easily flip the plane.

Dad went into a slow turn in a large arc, and as they slid past the mound in the snow, the wing missed it by inches. They looked at each other. Their obstacle was a snowman.

When the plane stopped, they were facing the compound, a little over a quarter mile away. An adult and two kids stood by the snowplow.

"We don't want to be exposed to them, even if they're not sick yet," Dad said. He got on the radio, but the school's unit was not on. Chad jumped out and waved at the people to move away from the truck. They went inside.

Chad climbed back in the plane. Dad kept the engines running and skimmed along the ground toward the snowplow.

"Wish we could just keep going like this all the way to Old Sparrow," Chad said.

"That would be nice," Dad said, "but we'd have to go airborne over every drift or mound. We'd never make it."

They looked at their watches. It was four o'clock, and the radio crackled to life. "This is Mike to December or whatever."

Chad smiled. "That's us."

"Mr. Quenton thinks the truck is about half full of gas. The gas pump is behind the kitchen at the end of the dining hall. He thinks you should try to put something heavy in the truck bed."

"We already thought of that," Chad said. "Is there a dirt pile or gravel somewhere?"

"There's some junk, old bed frames, and a sandpile near the barn. Shovels are in the barn."

"We'll try to make that work. Dad wants to know if the truck has chains on it."

"They're not on the tires, but they're in the truck, behind the seat. Mr. Quenton has one more request, but he wants to wait until you're ready to go."

"What is it?" Dad said, taking the radio.

"He doesn't want to tell you until the truck is gassed up, the truck bed loaded down, the chains on, and you're ready to pull out."

"What's the mystery?"

"I don't even know, sir," Mike said. "He said he'll try to make it out here to the radio to talk to you himself as soon as you're ready."

"Well, we should be ready to go in an hour or so. We'll come back to the radio in the plane at five."

"Okay. I mean, ten-four."

"Wait!" Chad said, leaning over the radio. "Just have Mr. Quenton speak to us from Kate's wrist TV."

"He and Kate aren't in the same room."

"Yeah, but it has to be easier to get the wrist TV to him than to get him up and to the radio."

"Good point. Five o'clock then?"

"Well," Dad said, "get him the radio now, and we'll call him when we're ready. If we can get away from here before five, we want to."

Dad signed off, and they climbed out.

Dad used deicer to startle the truck engine into waking up. The thing barely turned over but then rumbled noisily and finally caught. Dad backed it up, slipping and sliding, to the gas pump, where he filled it and told Chad he had left very little fuel for the generator. "We'll have to be quick and successful," he said.

Chad began shoveling sand and throwing junk into the open bed of the truck. It was hard, cold, miserable work, but he knew it was important. Dad left the truck running, and they jumped inside to get warm every few minutes.

A half hour later, Dad had the tire chains draped over the tires and was ready to hook them together. He told Chad how to drive the truck forward just a few inches, so he could link the chains. It took several tries, because the truck was a stick shift and Chad had to put in the clutch and shift every time he wanted to move the truck. But by quarter to five, they were ready to roll.

Dad and Chad sat up in the cramped cab of the truck, trying to keep the heater working correctly. Chad got on his wrist TV. "Mr. Quenton," he radioed. "Are you there?"

"I'm here," Mr. Quenton managed, his voice weak. "How do you work this thing?"

"Just press the upper right button to speak and let go to listen."

"Bruce?" Hugh Quenton called.

"Go ahead, Hugh," Dad said.

"I need a big favor." Chad heard the tremble in his voice.

"I'm listening."

"I need you to take Sue with you."

Over the River

"Repeat please?" Dad said into his wrist TV while glancing at Chad.

"I know it's a lot to ask," Mr. Quenton began, "and I know I'm putting you at tremendous risk. But this bug has wreaked havoc with Sue's blood-sugar levels, and she took her last dose of insulin this morning. We don't know when you might get to Old Sparrow or when you'll get back, but she'll need the insulin as soon as you can get to it."

"No options?" Dad said. "This cab is cramped and drafty."

"I don't see any options, Bruce. You know I wouldn't ask if I wasn't desperate."

"I know. Do you have surgical masks we could wear?"

"I think we could find a couple for you, and we'll put one on her too. Problem is, you'll have to be careful even opening them, because someone here will have to touch the boxes."

"Can Suzie Q get out here by herself?"

"We'll get her to the door. She's pretty weak, but she has eaten a little and she's medicated the best we know how. We'll bundle her up. Hopefully she'll sleep. Will you take her?"

"Of course. But I hate to think what might happen if we get stranded. One of us will have to stay with her."

"Bruce, if there were any other way …"

"I understand."

"One thing we know for sure," Mr. Quenton said, his voice breaking. "If we have to wait any longer than necessary, she runs the risk of a diabetic coma … and then almost certain death."

Chad glanced at his dad, who pressed his lips together and seemed to be fighting his own tears. "We'll do everything we can, Hugh."

"I know you will. But she must have the insulin as soon as you can get it. And of course, the rest of us need the antibiotics as soon as you can get back."

"Gotcha," Dad said. "You'd better get her out here as soon as you can."

Chad and Dad sat in the idling truck for a few minutes, trying to stay warm and watching the door at the back of the dining hall. "When she gets here," Dad said, "let's put her between us so she can stay warm."

"There's room for her to lie down behind the seat," Chad said.

Dad looked back. "It's bare metal on the floor, Chad, and we'll be bouncing. I wouldn't even want you there, and you're healthy."

The door opened and Suzie Q emerged slowly, a student on either side guiding her out, then letting go of her arms. She took slow, seemingly painful steps and stared at the truck, not turning her head. She wore a surgical mask and carried two more in small boxes.

Dad jumped out of his side of the truck and motioned for Chad to do the same. Dad took the two boxes from Suzie Q. He gave one of the boxes to Chad and told him to get out the mask and put it on. Dad put his own on, and the three of them climbed into the truck.

At one time, Chad could never have endured sitting that close to Suzie Q, but she seemed so fragile and he felt so sorry for her that he really didn't mind. He just wanted her to feel better, to get well, and to get the medicine she needed. He didn't know what a diabetic coma was, and he didn't want to find out.

Besides, Suzie Q had been nice to him the other morning, and he thought Kate might be right about Suzie Q growing up. She was friendly and pretty, and she really seemed to care about other people. All that silliness he remembered seemed to be gone.

The three of them sat in the truck, shoulder to shoulder, lap belts fastened, and Suzie Q had said nothing yet. “Do you mind if we call you Suzie Q?” Dad said. “We notice your parents don’t call you that anymore, and I assume you don’t go by that nickname here at the school. But it’s a hard habit for us to break.”

“Actually, I kind of like it, Mr. Michaels,” Susie Q spoke softly. “Only the people who knew us in Enid call me that, so it takes me home in my mind.”

“Then Suzie Q it is, at least for this trip. Are you going to be all right?”

“I’m feeling a little queasy, actually,” she said. “I’ll let you know if I have to throw up. You think maybe I should sit by the window with Chad in the middle?”

“It’s pretty cold by that window, hon.” Dad said, smiling. “We’ll move fast if you get sick.”

“I’m freezing already,” she said. “I think I can let you know in time for Chad to get out of my way.”

Chad laughed, and he could see from Suzie Q’s crinkled eyes above her mask that she was smiling.

“I’m so tired,” she said.

“You need anything right now?” Dad said.

"No, let's just go."

Dad depressed the clutch and shifted into low gear. The truck groaned and lurched as he let out the clutch and the gears engaged. The old beast rumbled slowly around the building and up the drive, heading toward the main road. The truck rattled and shook and bounced even where the road was fairly smooth, so Chad could only imagine what would happen when they tried to blast their way through heavy snowdrifts.

Suzie Q, her arms folded in front of her, tried to stay steady, but she tipped and swayed and would catch herself by grabbing the dashboard or leaning on either Chad or Dad. And she kept apologizing.

"Suzie Q," Dad said, "if you apologize every time you bump either of us, you'll never shut up. Let's just all apologize at once here and let it stand for the whole trip, okay?"

She laughed. "Sorry."

"There you go again. Now hang on."

They were near the end of the drive and about to pull out onto the highway, which was covered with about two feet of snow for as far as Chad could see. "I need a little speed here," Dad said, "and we're about to make a sharp left. Hang on."

Suzie Q braced herself on the dashboard, but as Dad picked up speed, downshifted, and hurtled the plow onto the road, all three passengers were thrown to the right. Suzie Q was pressed against Chad, pushing him toward the door. His head was plastered up against the iced-over window, and he expected his door to fly open.

Susie Q looked at him and started to say something.

"Don't apologize!" he hollered. "I understand!"

The truck straightened, they all sat up, and off they went down the road at between twenty-five and thirty miles an hour, bouncing like a crazy carnival ride. Twice Chad's head hit the ceiling, and he saw Dad press his left hand up there to make sure he didn't do the same. Suzie Q bounced up and down and up and down but didn't reach the ceiling because she was shorter than Chad. Once, though, when one bounce coincided perfectly with the next, all three of them were in the air, their seats off the bench, when the next bump came. They came down as the truck came up, and the bounce threw all three of them straight up into the ceiling of the cab. As they tumbled back down, Dad's foot slipped off the gas and the engine died.

"Oh, no!" Suzie Q cried.

"It's all right," Dad said. "I just lost contact." He turned the key, and after a few grinds on the engine, it fired up again. "Everybody all right?" Dad said.

Chad and Suzie Q looked at each other and nodded.

"Dad," Chad said, "I'm afraid I'm going to take this mask off and take my chances."

"Why?"

"It stinks. The smell is making me sick. I may be the first one who throws up."

"They do smell awful, don't they?" And Dad tore his off. Chad immediately followed, and Suzie Q asked if she could get rid of hers too.

"I think it's safe to say they weren't helping much anyway," Dad said. "Let's just hope God protects us, or you're already past the contagious stage."

For the next hour they chugged along. Sometimes the drifts were so large that Dad had to lower the plow and make his own path. Other times he engaged the snowblower and sent showers of dirt and ice and snow high into the air. Twice Suzie Q thought she might have to throw up. She whipped off her seat belt and climbed over Chad, hanging her head out the hastily lowered window, but both times were false alarms.

"It's all this bouncing," she said.

"I wish I could make it smoother," Dad said.

"I understand," she said. "There's no easy way to do this."

Finally they came to a mound of snow in the road that the plow couldn't budge. Dad tried attacking the seven-foot drift from two different directions with both the plow and the snowblower. "It would take at least two trucks and maybe more," he said. "I can't see them opening this for days."

"What are we going to do?" Suzie Q said.

"I'm going to have to go off the road for a while," Dad said. "That's why we weighted down the truck bed and put the chains on. I just hope this old buggy can make it through."

Dad downshifted to low again and turned off the roadway. The heavy truck plunged down a ravine and up the other side, as he kept clutching and shifting and punching the accelerator. For several minutes Dad drove as if on an obstacle course, looking for the points of least resistance. They weren't moving that fast, but it seemed they would never stop jostling up and down. Dad tore through fields, avoiding the deepest drifts, and when a shallow spot looked smooth, he drove right through it, even though it was clear they were hitting rocks, tree stumps, and even half-buried fence posts along the way.

For a ten-minute period, the way seemed almost smooth. The snow was only about a foot deep for a few miles, and Dad took the opportunity to increase his speed and make up some time. It wouldn't be long before nightfall, and he told Chad and Suzie Q that he didn't want to be driving in unfamiliar terrain after dark.

"How will we get back then?" Suzie Q said.

"That'll be easier. Well, not easier. Certainly not much smoother. But we will have been there before. We'll go back the exact way we came. All this work now is building us a path for the way back."

"As long as it doesn't get snowed under or drifted over," Suzie Q said.

"Hey!" Dad said. "None of that kind of thinking!"

And she smiled.

But soon, Suzie Q was asleep. She seemed to conk out in an instant, just as Chad was trying to think of something to talk to her about. One minute she was hanging onto the dashboard and occasionally slamming into him, and the next her arms lay limp in her lap, she was flopping back and forth, and her head was hanging.

"Is she all right, Dad?"

Dad looked at her. "Exhausted, I would guess. Her color looks all right. You could put your arm around her though, Spitfire. Otherwise she's going to bang into something."

"Dad!"

"Chad, it doesn't mean anything. I promise not to tell anyone. I'd put my arm around her, but I need one hand to shift with."

Chad looked at Suzie Q. He'd never sat with his arm around anyone except his parents. "Do it!" Dad said. "She won't even be aware of it, and she's going to get hurt if you don't!"

Chad reluctantly put his arm up behind Suzie Q on the back of the seat, but he didn't touch her. "Thatta boy!" Dad said, obviously not realizing that Chad still didn't have ahold of her. They hit a bump, and Suzie Q bounced toward Chad. He grabbed her shoulder and held tight, keeping her from banging into the dashboard or lurching back toward Dad. He still felt uncomfortable, but it wasn't anything romantic, after all.

The longer they sat like that and the more progress Dad made pushing the plow through the snow, the more brave and protective Chad felt. Suddenly Suzie Q's body went limp and she leaned over, settling in against Chad, her head on his chest. Whoops! This was more than he'd bargained for. He didn't know what to do, so he just sat there, his arm still around her shoulder.

"Dad?" he said.

"Just hang onto her," Dad said. "She's not going to bite you, and it's not going to kill you."

Chad whispered, "If she wakes up, she'll be embarrassed."

"Hm?" Dad said.

Chad didn't want to say it again, and certainly not loudly enough to wake her.

"Nothing," he said.

Suddenly Dad slammed on the brakes, and Chad hung onto Suzie Q tighter to keep her from flying forward.

"What?" Chad said.

Dad shook his head. "Look at this. And we were making such good progress. I'm guessing we're halfway there."

Chad stared out at a wall of snow. It stood higher than the truck as far as they could see to the left. To the right it extended all the way to the frozen-over and snow-filled Porcupine River. There was no way they could remove it or go through it.

"Do we have to go back, Dad?"

"I hope not."

He backed up and turned so he could flash his headlights far to the left. Nothing but a wall of snow. He turned to the right. The wall ended only at the river bank. "We've got to try it," Dad said.

"Try what?"

"Crossing the river. This is a mighty heavy truck, but that river isn't deep and has to be solid ice. It should hold us."

"Dad!"

Dad pointed across the river. "There's a woods on the other side where the snow has to be shallower. If we can pick our way through there, we'll be on our way to Old Sparrow."

He drove to the river's edge and eased the truck over the bank. It rolled and hurtled toward the ice, which seemed to hold it without any trouble. Dad drove straight across, which took only a few minutes. "We'll have to cross back again at some point," Dad reminded Chad, "because Old Sparrow is on the other side at the fork where the Porcupine splits. But we'll make it."

As they drew close to the other side and saw the woods looming, it became obvious that the bank was steeper on that side. Dad shifted and accelerated, and when the front tires hit the other side, the truck flew through the air, dumping half the weight from its bed and sending the debris sliding down the frozen river.

They settled back down and headed for the woods, but the jarring didn't even wake Sue. "Dad," Chad said, as he studied her, "Something's really wrong."

And through the Woods

Dad put the snowplow in neutral and set the brake. He turned on the inside light and leaned close to look at Suzie Q. She was pale, her eyelids fluttering, her lips bluish.

"Is she just cold?" Chad said.

"I don't think so," Dad said. "And I'm afraid this is more than whatever flu bug is going around."

"Does she need that diabetes medicine her dad talked about?"

"Insulin? Probably. I know a little about this because my grandmother was dependent on insulin. I haven't got time to explain it all to you now, but because her body is not producing insulin, her blood-sugar level is too high."

"Mr. Michaels," Suzie whispered weakly, obviously trying to focus on his face, "I've never needed insulin this badly in my life. If I don't get some soon, then ..."

"Then what?" Chad said.

"You don't want to know," she said.

"Yes, I do."

"My heart could fail. I could go into a coma and have a stroke. It wouldn't be good." She struggled to sit up. "Mr. Michaels, don't worry about making me sicker or bouncing me around. If there's insulin in Old Sparrow, we have to get there soon."

That was all Dad needed to hear. He lowered the snow-plow, turned on the noisy snowblower, shifted into low, punched the accelerator, and popped the clutch. The big old truck tires and chains dug into the snow and earth, and they began bouncing through the woods.

It was dark in among the trees, and Chad wondered how his dad could see far enough ahead to make his turns. The snowblower rattled and squealed as it ground up twigs and branches and pushed huge mounds of snow off to the side. Dad would get the truck up to twenty-five or thirty miles an hour, pushing big drifts ahead of him, then he would raise the plow and the truck would run up the pile in the way, bounce down the other side, and keep going.

Chad put both hands on the lap belt across his lap and held on. Suzie Q was bouncing all over. She grabbed the dashboard, but her hands flew loose. She pressed her palms flat on the ceiling to try to keep from hitting her head.

"You sure you're all right?" Dad shouted as he shifted and clutched and turned and plowed.

"Yes," she shouted. "Keep going!"

Chad thought he saw a clearing at the other edge of the woods, but just before the opening was a rim of short, thin trees. The thickest might have been five inches around, and they were no more than fifteen feet tall.

Dad jerked the truck this way and that, avoiding big trees, dipping into holes, and sideswiping medium-sized trees. With the clearing in sight, he lifted the plow, turned off the blower, and shifted into high gear. The truck was flying. Dad, Suzie Q, and Chad were bouncing around and banging into each other. They must have been going nearly forty miles an hour through underbrush and between trees in the snow.

Ten feet from the last of the big trees, Dad came full throttle to the rim of thin saplings encircling the forest and suddenly had nowhere to turn. The truck couldn't fit between the small trees, and Dad was going too fast to stop. He bore down, ran over two small trees, and then hit a slightly bigger one head on.

The tree nearly stopped the truck. The force of the old machine as it rolled over the tree almost bent it all the way to the ground, but while the plow tore the bark from the trunk to the branches, the truck was barely moving. The tree rumbled and scraped beneath it, as if struggling to straighten itself again. As the truck rolled forward, the tree lifted the back tires into the air, and nearly flipped the truck over frontward.

Chad saw the snowy ground out the windshield directly below him and was certain they were about to flip end over end. He hung on, Suzie screamed, Dad grunted, and the tree slid to one side of the underbelly of the truck and made them tip to Chad's side. Now they were about to roll that way, and Chad wondered if he would wake up in heaven. Who would take care of Kate? Would he see his mother? What would the Quentons think? Who would ever find them in these woods? What if more snow covered their tracks and even the truck? They might lie frozen in this thing for days!

As Chad thought about all this, somehow the truck righted itself and bounced down on both axles, the four tires in the back and the two in the front now solidly in the snow again. Dad had never taken his foot off the accelerator, so the back wheels had spun at top speed while suspended by the little tree beneath them. When they again hit the ground, they dug a huge hole and shot the truck forward even faster.

Suzie Q hollered, "Go! Go!"

Chad's heart banged inside his chest, and he tried to stop thinking about how they might die. As Dad took a hard left to head back to the Porcupine River, which he would have to cross again to get to Old Sparrow, Suzie Q was thrown almost into Chad's lap. Only her lap belt kept her from landing on him.

As she was flung into him again, he felt a strange lack of tension in her body; she was either spent or had given up trying to protect herself from the bouncing. Her infection and her diabetes must have sapped all her strength. Chad put his arm around her again, and she settled against him, her mittened hands clasped in her lap.

If he didn't hold onto her, she would be thrown all over the cab and could really hurt herself. Suzie Q was awake, and sometimes Chad sensed her eyes on him from close range, as her head bounced up and down on his chest. He was embarrassed and a little uncomfortable, but he kept one arm around her shoulder and the other firmly on the dashboard.

"Everybody all right?" Dad said, not taking his eyes off the path he was creating.

"Yeah," Chad said.

"Suzie Q?"

"Yup, I'm still here," she said.

"I figure we're about four miles from Old Sparrow. If I keep getting lucky and finding places to push this rig, we should be there inside half an hour."

"This isn't luck, Mr. Michaels," Suzie Q said. "I'm praying my heart out."

"Me too," Dad said. "You're right."

Dad was now pushing the snowplow through a field covered with a shallow layer of snow, and though it was not a paved road, it seemed more bouncy than it should have been. "Dad," Chad said, "are we bouncing even more than before, especially in the back?"

"Could be," Dad said, searching for the best spot to cross the frozen Porcupine again. "I don't know how much weight we lost out of the truck bed."

"I'll check," Chad said, lowering his window. Suzie Q dropped her head and put her hands up to cover her face against the blast of cold air and snow. Chad pulled his arm away from her shoulder, and she sat up, allowing him room to turn and crouch on the seat. He thrust his head and torso out the window and stood on the seat, squinting and peering over the back of the trailer.

Chad slithered back into the cab and shut the window. "Empty," he said.

"Completely?" Dad said. "That explains the bouncing."

The truck chugged along, rattling and bouncing, and Chad automatically put his arm around Susie Q again so she wouldn't go flying. She settled in, leaning against him, her hands in her lap. He wouldn't have wanted anyone else but Dad to see him in this predicament. Certainly not Kate or any of his friends.

"Once we get across the Porcupine again, we can head for the road and see if it's any better," Dad said. "I'd sure like to get into Old Sparrow on the main drag."

Dad pulled the truck near the bank of the river, but it was hard to tell where the field ended and the drop-off to the ice began, because of the drifting snow. He must have seen a good entry point then, because he angled the truck to the left and rumbled down toward the river. Chad kept expecting to hear cracking ice and then the gurgling sound of a sinking truck.

But the truck rode the smoothest since they had left the Christian school. In some spots on the river the snow was only six inches deep, so if Dad maintained the right speed, they sailed along, the tires cutting through the snow and the chains biting into the surface of the ice.

"Do you trust the river?" Chad said.

"Sure! Why not?" Dad said. "Ice has to be a couple of feet thick. It's been frozen over for a month, and the temperatures up here have averaged below zero for weeks."

"I don't know," Chad said. "Just gives me the creeps being over water in this heavy thing."

Suzie Q seemed to be sleeping. Her eyes were closed, her body relaxed, and her breathing even and deep. He looked close to make sure her eyelids were not fluttering or her lips blue. She looked fine. Maybe this was best for her. She was sick, out of diabetes medicine, and exhausted. Now, if he could keep her from getting bruised up on this crazy ride ...

"There's the highway." Dad pointed ahead and to his left. "It actually looks passable, though it hasn't been plowed in a while. I'm going to try to get over there."

The bank on the left side looked steeper than where they had slid down onto the river. They needed to find a gentle slope and gather enough speed to make it up. Chad pointed out a spot about two hundred yards ahead. "Does that look good?" he said.

"From here it does," Dad said, and he increased his speed, angling toward the place.

Chad noticed underbrush above the snow line, something he rarely saw in northern Alaska or Canada. The exit area was looking better all the time.

Dad maneuvered the truck into position to shoot up the shallow slope and onto the bank. He accelerated, then suddenly he slammed on the brakes, sending the truck into a skid. What had appeared to be a short snow bank was really a boulder! If Dad hit it at top speed, they'd be killed!

The truck slid in a straight line. Dad quickly let off the brake so the front tires would roll, then he jerked the wheel to the right. The tires were turned, but still the truck slid forward. When they were just a few feet from hitting the boulder head on, the truck finally slowed enough and, following the direction of the tires, lurched to the right.

The truck went into a huge slide, missing the boulder but cutting a huge circle through the snow and on the ice. Chad felt as if he might pass out as they spun around and around. He held tight to Suzie Q, who did not budge or awaken.

This would have been fun if Dad had done it on purpose. Of course, had they not been on ice, anything they'd hit during this kind of spin would have tipped them over and spilled them out.

The truck finally came to a stop, and there they sat in the middle of the frozen-over Porcupine River, not far from the U.S. Canadian border, a few miles from Old Sparrow. Again Chad imagined the ice cracking and that monstrous old snowplow sinking slowly into the frigid waters with him and his dad and his friend inside.

Friend. Yes, that was what Suzie Q was now.

Dad shifted into low gear but had difficulty getting the tire chains to move slowly enough to gain traction on the ice. Finally they were moving again, and Chad could see that just upriver was an opening. If Dad could generate enough speed and there were no more hidden rocks, they just might be able to make it out of here alive.

Facing the Wall

As they bounced up the bank and then turned toward the highway, Chad wondered what this crazy ride was doing to his spine, not to mention his dad's or Suzie Q's. At any other time, he might have thought this was fun, but after a couple hours of it, he had had enough. It was noisy, it was painful, it was cold, and he was still embarrassed sitting there with his arm around Suzie Q as if they were a couple.

Dad steered the truck off the plains and through some drifts onto the highway. The snow was deep, and there was no evidence that any cars or trucks had driven along the road for hours. Occasionally they passed a car or truck in the ditch or at a crazy angle at the side of the road, buried under the snow. But finally, for the first time, they seemed to be making good time. For about five minutes, Dad averaged thirty miles an hour.

Chad caught Dad straining and looking puzzled as he stared into the distance. “What?” Chad said.

“Is that what it looks like?” Dad said. “Or is it my imagination?”

Chad leaned forward and scraped the film of frost off the inside of the windshield. He couldn’t believe his eyes.

“Have you ever seen anything like that?” Dad said.

Chad couldn’t speak. He just shook his head and stared. He had walked all night through snowdrifts to get home. He had ridden in an ancient snowplow across drifted plains, through the woods, and across a frozen river twice. But Chad had never before seen what lay ahead of them—a wall of snow twice as high as the truck stretched across the entire highway, plus as far as he could see on either side of it.

It was as if someone had recreated the Great Wall of China out of snow. “So that’s what happens when three storm fronts converge.” Dad took his foot off the gas and allowed the truck to roll slowly, closer and closer to the wall of snow. He stopped about a hundred feet from the blockage and looked to the left and to the right. “There’s flat nowhere to go,” he said. “I can’t believe we’ve come this far and can go no farther.”

Chad looked both ways as well. There was no going around this thing.

His dad laid his arms on the steering wheel. "It looks like the twister-type winds from one storm hit the same winds from another storm, while the third storm provided the snow."

Chad was almost afraid to ask. "How far are we from Old Sparrow?"

"Not more than a mile," Dad said with a sigh. "So close."

Suzie Q awoke. "What's happening?"

"Look," Chad said.

"Oh, man!" she said. "What are we going to do?"

"There's nothing we can do in this truck," Dad said. "I'm going to have to try to walk around or over this thing." Dad reached behind the seat for his snowshoes. He slathered a huge dollop of petroleum jelly all over his face, tightened his hood, zipped and buttoned and snapped everything that could be fastened on his snowmobile suit, tossed the snowshoes out on the ground, and stepped out. As he struggled into the snowshoes, he said, "Chad, keep your wrist TV on, and I'll let you know how it goes."

Chad noticed Suzie Q's hands shaking. "Cold?" he said.

"Nervous," she said. "Terrified actually. I don't have much time. Mr. Michaels, I can wait here if you need Chad to go with you."

"I couldn't do that, hon," Dad said. "I'll be worried enough about the two of you without worrying about you alone. I don't know what Chad's going to do if you have another crisis, but we sure can't leave you alone out here. There's plenty of gas to keep the heater going, and I'll go as fast as I can."

Dad leaned in and turned the heat all the way up. When he shut the door the cab began to get warm, and Suzie slid over behind the wheel. "Thanks for keeping me warm," she said.

Chad felt his face flush. "You're welcome."

"While the truck's not moving, it's not so drafty, so I'm okay now."

"Good!" he said. "I mean, I didn't mind, I mean, it was all right, but—"

"I understand," she said, laughing. "You never expected to have to keep your old enemy warm."

"You're not my enemy," Chad said.

"I used to be."

"Not really."

"Now tell the truth, Chad. You always thought I was a little brat."

Chad turned toward the window to watch his dad. "Yeah, I guess I did."

Dad looked left and right, and then headed straight up the wall of snow. Climbing in snowshoes was no easy task, but there was obviously no other way to get up there.

He fell twice and rolled once and had to come back down another time to retrieve a snowshoe. But finally he reached the summit.

"Chad, come in, please," came Dad's staticky voice on Chad's wrist.

"I read you," Chad said.

"Look at this." Dad turned his wrist to give Chad a blurry, LCD readout view of what he saw from the top of the wall of snow. Chad showed Suzie Q.

They both said, "Wow."

"It's hard to see, Dad," Chad said, "but it looks like that would be a great place for a sled."

"Wish I had a toboggan," Dad said. "It just angles down for a quarter of a mile or so, and it looks like you can almost see pavement at the end. The road looks passable, but I don't see anyone coming this way. They've probably got all their snow-removal equipment in town, trying to dig out. This will take a week."

"Should be easy walking though, right, Dad?"

"Hope so. This seems firm enough, so by the time I get to the road I should be able to make good time. You guys all right?"

"Yeah." Chad watched his dad start down the other side of the wall of snow. He didn't want to worry Suzie Q, but if that snow wasn't as firm as his dad hoped, he could drop through and be buried alive.

"Suzie Q?" Dad said. "You okay?"

"Yes, sir," she said, leaning over to talk into the little contraption on Chad's wrist. "I'm fine for now. I'll sure feel better when I know you're on your way back with the insulin."

"Me too," he said. The picture on the TV screen disappeared. It was toasty now in the cab of the truck, yet Chad still shivered. When was the last time he had sat in an enclosed place with a girl other than his sister and had to carry on some kind of intelligent conversation?

"I was a brat," Suzie Q said. "I was jealous of Kate because she had a brother, so I pretended I didn't like you and tried to make life miserable for you."

"You were pretending?"

"I had just decided I didn't like boys, that boys weren't as good as girls, and so I did everything I could to annoy you."

"You succeeded. To tell you the truth, I couldn't stand you."

"I don't blame you. I don't know what was wrong with me then. Maybe I was feeling sorry for myself because of my diabetes. When I was eight, I had to start giving myself my own insulin shots."

"Yuck."

"Yuck is right. I'm used to it now and I know how important it is, but it's never been fun, never anything you'd wish on anyone."

"Has the diabetes kept you from doing things you want to do?"

"Not really. I have to be careful what I eat and when I eat, and I have to keep track of my blood-sugar levels. I stick my finger, and then a little machine measures the glucose in my blood. Honestly, I hate doing that all the time, even more than I hate giving myself the shots."

"I'd hate to have to do either one."

"Don't feel sorry for me though. I don't want pity."

Chad nodded. "I can understand that. Kate and I got a lot of pity when Mom died."

"I felt sorry for you too," Suzie Q said.

"That's fine, but we're trying to do what Dad does. He remembers the good times and talks about her all the time. We know she's in heaven, and we can't wait to see her someday."

"See, that's sort of how I feel about my diabetes now. My parents are always trying to find positive things about it. With my mom being a nurse, well, what could be better than that? When I was younger, she did everything for me. She sang and talked to me about fun stuff to get my mind off the shots."

"You have to do that every day?" Chad said.

Suzie Q gave a tired smile. "I get four shots per day on a normal day, usually when I eat my meals."

"Four! You get the shots in the leg, huh?"

"Yeah. Usually above the knee, or on the arm or even the stomach. It has to be a place where there's more fatty tissue."

"It doesn't hurt?"

"Not bad. I'm so used to it. The needles are tinier than they've ever been and are getting sharper all the time. Sometimes they slip in so easily I really don't feel them." She sighed. "I think I hate watching my diet more than anything. Hardly any junk food or sugar allowed."

Chad turned to face her. "Have you ever gone this long without insulin before?"

"I don't think so. I mean, actually I have, but I didn't need it as much. The older I get, the more I need. And if I get tense or upset or sick, then I need more. That's the problem right now. I had enough insulin to last a few normal days, but with being sick, and then the blizzard and everybody else getting sick, I had a couple of close calls."

Chad scowled. "What if you have another one of those?"

She shrugged. "You never know. Once when playing softball, I was waiting to hit, and I felt this tingling in my tongue and in my fingers. That was a sign I was having circulation problems because of my blood-sugar level. But I ignored it—stupid thing to do—and hit the ball hard. I hit a home run!"

"Couldn't you have called time out?"

"I could have, but it would have been so embarrassing. I just moved into the batter's box, hoping the pitcher would give me anything close. The first pitch I could reach I blasted over the left fielder's head. I ran so fast around those bases I think she had just gotten to the ball when I was rounding third. Everybody thought I was running so fast because I wanted a homer.

"My teammates were all waiting to slap my hand at the plate, but I just ran right through them. I was so excited and pumped, but I was shaking bad. Mom just reached over the fence and gave me my shot, right through my uniform pant leg."

"You can do that?"

"You're not supposed to. It's not the most sanitary. But time is what's most important." She paused. "Chad? Will you forgive me?"

"Forgive you?"

"For being such a brat when we were little and then for never apologizing before now? I had lots of chances, with all those emails I've sent to Kate. I'm sorry."

"It's all right."

"Then you accept my apology?"

"Sure."

"You think we can be friends?"

Chad smiled. "As long you don't tell anybody."

"Well, it's not like we'd be boyfriend and girlfriend or anything like that," she said.

"I know, but I don't have any other friends who are girls."

"That makes me special," Suzie Q said.

"That's not all that makes you special." Chad could hardly believe he'd said that.

"What?" she said.

"Nothing."

"Don't say 'nothing.' I heard what you said. What did you mean?"

"Nothing, now really. Please."

"Chad, come in, please," Dad said over his wrist TV, and Chad sighed with relief.

Crisis in Old Sparrow

"Go ahead, Dad."

"Chad? I've run into trouble here. I'm in Old Sparrow, and it looks as much like a ghost town down here as it did from the air. They've got snow-removal equipment trying to clear the main drag, but it has huge drifts. Power is still out, everything's closed up. I just went over to the drugstore, and it's sealed up tight. I'm going to have to hunt down the pharmacist and find out where his shipment of medicine is."

"Ten-four," Chad said. "I can't see you, by the way."

"Well, it's dark here already. Anyway, the high frequency radio waves will not go through that snow mountain you've got in front of you, Chad," Dad said. "The low frequency transmitter Kate built into these things works fine from this distance."

"Ten-four."

"How's Suzie Q doing?"

"She's a little shaky. I should let her speak for herself."

"I'm trying to hold up," Suzie said into Chad's wrist transmitter, "but I don't know how much longer I can make it."

"I'm coming as fast as I can, Suzie."

"Thanks."

Just talking about Suzie's condition made Chad nervous. But he'd rather talk about that than what he had stupidly brought up a minute before about her being special. Why had he even said that in the first place?

A few minutes later Chad realized that Dad had left his transmitter on. They heard his steps and even his heavy breathing as he fought his way through the elements looking for someone in Old Sparrow to talk to. But just as Chad was about to signal Dad and tell him to turn off his sending mechanism, he heard conversation.

"Evening, gentlemen," Chad's dad said. "Might have guessed the only place open in town would be the bar." He was met with whistles and shrieks and laughter. "How you keeping warm?"

"Hooch!" somebody hollered. "Booze! Have yourself one!"

"No, thanks," Dad said. "Those heaters safe?"

"Who knows? We'd be dead without 'em."

"Listen, I'm looking for the pharmacist. Anybody know where he is? His place is closed."

That was met with more laughter and shouting. Then Dad said, "Who? You?"

Apparently the pharmacist had been pointed out to his dad. Chad heard footsteps again, then, "Hey, there, partner, you awake? Sit up here a minute. I hate to wake you or bother you, but do you remember me?"

"Remember you? No! Leave me alone."

"I wish I could, but I can't. I was in your store the other day, looking to pick up a shipment of medical supplies, antibiotics, and insulin. Remember? C'mon, pal, stay with me a minute here. The Old Sparrow Christian School got word the shipment had arrived here, and that's why I came. People are sick back there. We need it bad, and we need it now."

"I got cleaned out," the man said. "Looted, you understand? My burglar alarm wasn't working, and somebody came in and cleaned me out."

"What are you talking about?" Dad said. "I was just by your place and it was locked up tight."

"So that wasn't my place that got busted into?"

Chad glanced at Suzie Q. Every minute counted, and they were losing critical time.

After another chorus of laughs, somebody said, "You from that Christian school?"

"Yes, sir, I am."

"Well, they reached somebody on the shortwave a little while ago over at the station. They were looking for you, saying you were going to be in town this afternoon and to give you a message."

"What's the message?"

"Something about they still need the medicine and all, but some of them are starting to get better, and they don't see it as life-threatening or anything."

"That's great news. Anything else?"

"No, but they wanted to hear from you as soon as you got here."

"I can talk to them from the gas station?"

"They're closed—everybody's working on the roads and power and such."

"Not *everybody*," Dad said, obviously referring to the drinkers in front of him. "None of you guys willing to pitch in and help?"

"This was an act of nature," somebody yelled. "We didn't have nothin' to do with it."

"So you're just going to roll over and let everyone else do the cleanup work? Now as for you," and Chad knew he must be talking to the pharmacist again, "you're coming with me and opening your store."

"And what if I don't?" the man slurred.

"Then I'll break into your place and find the stuff. I've got an emergency situation, and I've got to have that medicine."

"I just heard him tell you it wasn't a big deal anymore."

"I'm talking about the insulin," Dad said in a tight voice. "I need it right now. Either you come and give it to me, or I'll find a way to get in there."

"Oh, all right!" the man muttered, and Chad and Suzie Q heard him grumbling to himself as the men's boots crunched the frozen snow until they reached the drugstore. They heard the jangle of keys and a lot of fumbling around.

"Just show me which one it is and let me do it," Dad said in a disgusted tone.

Soon they heard the door open and the two clomp inside. "It's no warmer in here than it is out there," the pharmacist said.

"At least we're out of the wind," Dad said. "Now where's that shipment?"

"I don't know. It's here somewhere. I drove all the way to McDougall myself, you know, when that storm had just started. I was lucky to get back alive."

"I'd be more impressed if you were trying to dig your town out of this mess."

"Well, Sonny," the man said, "we all react to trouble in our own way, don't we?"

"I guess we do. Now if you're not going to look, tell me where to look. Where'd you put the stuff when you got back here?"

"You know, I don't remember bringing it in from the car."

"What are you saying? You left fresh medicine in the car to freeze?"

"Oh, don't get your mind in a bind. It comes in insulated boxes. It's all right."

"Well, let's go! Where's your car?"

"I didn't take the car. I took the truck."

"Then where's the truck? Come on, man! This is an emergency!"

"It's out back."

Chad looked at Suzie Q, who appeared weaker and more fidgety. She held up a hand, anticipating Chad's question. "I'm okay," she said.

Over the wrist TV they heard Dad's footsteps, firm and alone, out the door and into the snow again. "Hey there!" Dad said.

"Hello," came the voice of a young man.

"Name's Bruce Michaels."

"I'm Sam. My dad's the pharmacist here."

"Your dad's a heavy drinker."

"Don't I know it. What can I do for you?"

"He said a shipment of medicine is in this truck. A lot of it is for the Old Sparrow Christian School, and I'm getting it for them."

"You'll never get over there until they clear the highway, probably some time next week," Sam said. Dad quickly filled him in on how he had gotten there and about the urgent need for the insulin. "Well, then, let's find you that stuff and get you on your way."

Chad and Suzie Q heard them rooting around in the truck. "Nothing here," Sam said.

"Sam," Dad said. "This is an emergency. Maybe you can communicate to your father better than I can. I have got to have that stuff, and right away."

"I'll try."

"I'll wait here," Dad said.

They heard Sam move away and Dad said into his wrist TV, "Chad?"

"Yeah, Dad, we hear you. In fact we've heard everything since you were in the bar."

"It was the only business in town where I saw any smoke rising from the chimney. How's Suzie?"

"I'm fine," she called out, a little too loudly.

"To tell you the truth, I'm worried about her," Chad said.

"Why?" she screeched. "I'm fine! I said I was fine! I'm fine!"

"Suzie," Dad said. "You sound a little hyper."

"I'm not! I'm fine."

"Hurry, Dad," Chad said.

"Ten-four. Here comes Sam, and he doesn't look too pleased."

"Leave your watch on, Dad," Chad said quickly, but it was too late. The signal suddenly ended and the sound disappeared.

"Now what?" Suzie Q said. "Is he in trouble? I hope he's not in trouble, because if he's in trouble, I'm in trouble."

Chad sat back and stared at her.

"What?"

"Can you hear yourself?" he said. "Something's wrong with you. You talked normally after Dad left, but now you're totally wired."

Suzie began to cry.

"I'm sorry, Suzie, I didn't mean to upset you. It's just that—"

"No! It's that—I don't want to be this way. This is how I get when I'm not producing insulin and my blood is full of sugar!" She was still crying. "You're such a good friend, Chad."

"Yeah, okay."

"No! You are! Let me tell you what a good friend you are!"

"Okay, Suzie. Take it easy now. Dad will be back soon."

"You don't know that! We don't even know what happened to him!"

"Suzie, please, you have to calm down. My dad was a fighter pilot. He's been in every kind of situation you can imagine, and he can handle himself."

But Suzie wasn't listening. She covered her face with her mittens and rubbed her forehead, rocking back in the seat.

"Are you all right?" Chad said.

"I'm fine" came the muffled shout from behind the mittens. "I told you and your dad I'm fine, so I'm fine, okay?"

"Okay, okay. Sorry."

Suddenly Suzie Q pulled her hands away from her face and spoke calmly and seriously. "Listen to me, Chad, I'm all screwed up with glucose and insulin. You can't take personally anything I might say or do, okay?"

"Okay."

"Promise? You understand?"

Chad nodded. "Suzie, listen to me," he said. "I completely understand, all right? Don't worry about anything. Just try to stay calm and stay warm, and let's pray my dad gets back here with your insulin."

The wrist TV crackled. "Chad, I'm on the street with Sam. His dad finally admitted he sold the stuff to some guy at the gas station."

"Sold it?" Chad shouted.

"Oh, no!" Suzie Q wailed.

"He wanted some money, and the guy said he would sell it to the rescue workers for a profit and split it with him."

"What are you going to do, Dad?"

"Sam's taking me to find the guy. I'll try to get on the radio back to the school."

"Why'd he sell the stuff when he knew it was the school's?"

"He said he knew we'd never make it to Old Sparrow."

"He didn't know us, did he, Dad?"

"Suzie hanging in there?" Dad said.

"Not really. She needs the stuff as soon as we can get it."

"Ten-four."

"And Dad, leave your TV on."

Suzie had buried her face in her mittens again and was rocking in the seat. What if she collapsed or lost consciousness? How would he know if it was a coma or whether she was dying? What if she had heart failure? It was more than he wanted to think about. All he knew was that he could not, *would not*, let her die.

He wanted her conscious when his dad returned with the medicine, because neither he nor his dad knew how to give her the injection. Sure, he had seen doctors and nurses use hypodermic needles before, but he certainly never thought he'd have to do it himself.

"How big a dose do you need?" Chad said, just in case.

"I need a lot," Suzie Q said, "but my first dose after a long time can't be more than thirty units, or it'll be too much for my system."

"Thirty units," he repeated.

They fell silent, and Chad listened desperately for his dad on his wrist TV.

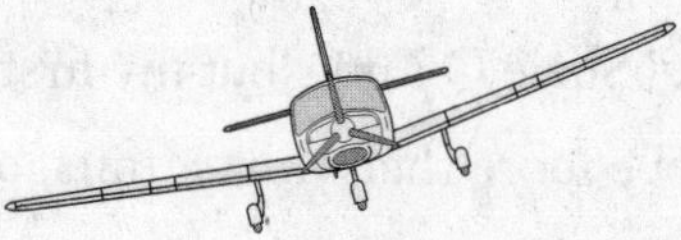

Racing the Clock

Suzie Q leaned back on the headrest and seemed to fall asleep, though her fingers were still moving and her hands shaking. On his wrist TV Chad suddenly heard Dad's new acquaintance, Sam, talking with someone at the gas station. Then he heard Dad on his shortwave radio to the Christian school.

"I have good news," Dad said. "We should be heading back soon." He told them where Chad and Suzie Q were. "Once I get the medicine, we'll be on our way. Ten-four. Over and out."

"Not so fast," someone was saying. "I didn't say I'd sell you the stuff."

"I don't have to buy it from you," Dad said. "It was ordered by the Christian school, and it's going on their bill."

"Then you don't even have the cash for it?"

"Like I said, it goes on the school's account."

"Then give me one reason I shouldn't just sell it to the rescue workers and make my profit in cash, like I planned."

"Because it's not yours to sell."

"I bought it from Sam's dad."

"You paid him already?" Sam said.

"I didn't say that. I'll pay him from the profits."

Sam's voice was like steel. "You heard this man say that the Christian school has a crisis and a little girl just outside town is gonna die if she doesn't get her medicine, and you're not going to do the right thing?"

"Sam, the right thing is none of your business. It's my stuff, and I'll make that decision."

Chad heard Sam whisper to Dad, "Are you prepared to run?"

"I'll do whatever I have to do, Sam, and I appreciate your help."

"Let me do this," Sam said, and Chad could tell by his loud voice that he was talking to the man with the medicine. "Let me check the supply and see what it's worth, and then we can talk about a proper price. Fair enough?"

"I guess," the other man said.

Chad was fascinated. He could only imagine what was going on. It was quiet for a minute, then Sam shouted,

"Go!" He heard fast footsteps, shouting, a door slamming, running, and finally, Dad.

"Chad! Chad! Come in please!"

"I'm here, Dad!" Chad said. "What's happening?"

Dad was clearly running; he was already panting. "I'm trying to get far enough from these yokels to get my snowshoes on."

"What's going on?"

"Sam got the stuff from the guy, handed it to me, and motioned that I should get going! We owe him a big thanks."

"Can you outrun those guys?"

"Sure!"

Chad heard a loud pop. "What was that? It sounded like a gun!"

"That's what it was," Dad said. "They can't catch me, so one of 'em's shooting!"

Chad shouted, "Leave your transmitter on!"

"I wish this case wasn't so heavy!" Dad said, his breath coming in short bursts.

Chad heard another shot. "Dad!"

"I'm all right! They're just trying to scare me. I have to keep moving! They can't even see me now!"

"Save your breath and just get here!"

"I'm coming!"

Chad couldn't believe what this trip had turned into. He could just see Dad lurching through town, trying to get back to the road where he would put on his snowshoes and climb the huge incline and then scamper down the other side to the snowplow. Dad had to still be a mile away, and while the lazy locals may have given up chasing him, he had to keep running. He must be exhausted. Chad thought about climbing to the top of the drift in the road to watch for him, but he couldn't leave Suzie Q.

He turned to her. "So what do you think about that?"

She didn't stir. She seemed to be sound asleep. How could she have slept through his yelling over the TV transmitter? Had she slipped into a coma? He felt for a pulse in her wrist. It was faint.

"Suzie Q? Are you all right?"

"Hm?" she said, still sounding asleep.

"Are you all right?"

He thought she nodded, but he wasn't sure. Maybe sleep was good. Maybe he should leave her alone. He didn't know how long it would take Dad to trudge back through the deep snow with the medicine.

"Chad!" Dad called.

"Go ahead."

"I'm on the outskirts of town, a little less than a mile from you. I'm going to rest here a second and get my snowshoes on."

"Dad, what was the good news from the school?"

"A lot of them are getting better. This thing was highly contagious, but it's only a forty-eight-hour bug. They still need the antibiotics, but they're encouraged."

"Good."

"I'm on the move again. How's Suzie Q?"

"She doesn't look good. She's sleeping. She doesn't seem to hear me."

"Does she look calmer than before?"

"I guess."

"Let her be, she just needs the insulin," Dad said. "Hang on till I get there."

What else could he do?

Chad heard the crunching of Dad's snowshoes, the steady, quick gait of a man in a hurry.

Suddenly Suzie Q turned, opened her eyes, and looked Chad full in the face. She seemed to want to say something, but nothing came out.

"You okay, Suzie?" Chad said.

She just continued to stare, as if she were sleeping with her eyes open.

"Suzie!" he said, louder this time.

"Chad," she said quietly.

"Yeah?"

"Chad?" she repeated.

"What, Suzie?"

"Do you know what CPR is?"

"Yeah."

"I mean, do you know how to do it?"

"Perform CPR, you mean?"

"Yes."

"Yeah, we learned in health last year. Why?"

"Because I think I need it."

"Are you kidding?"

But Suzie didn't answer. She just stared at Chad, not blinking. She coughed twice, causing her little body to bounce, but still she stared.

"Suzie Q! Are you serious? You need CPR?"

She didn't move and her eyes seemed to freeze. Her pupils were huge, and Chad wondered if that's what doctors on TV meant when they described someone's pupils as "fixed and dilated."

Now he was scared. What was he supposed to do? He felt for her pulse again, but this time he felt none. He put his ear to her mouth and heard nothing. *Had she died right in front of him?* He felt the pressure points beneath her lower jaw at the neck. Nothing!

"Suzie!"

Her head rolled to one side, and she began to topple. He grabbed her shoulders and she leaned heavily on him. Chad pulled his knees onto the seat and knelt there, trying to guide Suzie onto her back. But she was too close to the driver's side door. Chad scooted over to the other side and put his hands under her arms, pulling her across the seat on her back. He reached to open the passenger-side door, then stood on the step, leaning over her. She lay still, staring blankly at the ceiling.

"Suzie!" he yelled, then decided not to yell at her again. She couldn't hear him. The wind was icy, and the sky was dark, but suddenly Chad's life seemed to be moving in slow motion.

"God, help me!" Chad prayed. He flipped on his transmitter. "Dad! Hurry! I think Suzie's dying!"

"What's happening?" came the reply.

"No pulse, no breathing."

"Start CPR!"

"I will!"

"You know what to do. I'll get there as fast as I can!"

Suzie's knees were up, her boots pressing against the driver's side door. Chad needed to shut his own door or they would both freeze. He crawled inside and knelt with his back to the dashboard, facing the seat. He tugged on Suzie until she was stretched out before him, her head resting on the passenger seat. Then he shut the door.

Chad whipped off his gloves and tore at the buckle at her waist that kept her snowsuit tight around her. Once that was loose he untied the string under her chin and pulled down her hood. He bunched it up under her neck and moved her head back a little to keep the windpipe open.

Suzie went rigid now, her arms and legs straight. Her eyes were still open but lifeless. Her mouth was slightly open, her teeth clenched. Chad forced a finger between her teeth to open her air passage.

He unzipped her snowsuit to her waist, then tipped her head back and covered her mouth with his. He blew air into her until her cheeks puffed and her chest rose a little. Then he clasped his hands together and placed them just below her sternum. He pushed firmly but not too hard.

He alternated between forcing air into her lungs and pressing on her sternum, stopping every third time to listen for breathing or for a pulse.

"Anything?" Dad said over the transmitter. "Don't answer until you have a pulse. Don't take time out to talk to me unless you know you can."

"No!" Chad shouted.

"Keep working, Chad. I'm praying for you, and I know you can do this."

"What if she dies?" Chad squealed.

Dad sounded surprisingly calm. "You know what to do, so just keep doing it."

Chad could hear his dad gasping as he ran through the frozen wilderness. "I'm on the highway!" Dad said.

Chad couldn't respond. His own heart was pounding enough for both him and Suzie Q. He had to do something to get her breathing and to get her heart beating again. When he had taken CPR training he had hoped he would never have to use it. He'd wondered if he could, and he'd always hoped that someone else would be around who could do it instead.

Now he had no choice. Suzie Q's life depended on him. He breathed into her mouth, and he pushed against her breastbone. He looked for any signs of life. Her face was pale, her lips blue.

"C'mon, Suzie Q," he whispered. "C'mon!"

How long could she hang on with no heartbeat, with no air? He would never give up, but he wanted something to happen. "God, please!" he cried out.

He was massaging her heart when he sensed her body relax a little. Her arm moved! When he tried to breathe for her again, she turned her head and sputtered.

"Suzie!"

He felt for a pulse. It was faint. And then it was gone, and he began again. Several times he felt he had brought her back, only to lose her again. He was panicky, but he would not lose control. He couldn't. He had to hang on.

"Dad!" he called. "I don't know if I'm doing any good!"

"As long as you're doing anything," Dad said between gasps, "you're doing good. Keep it up!"

"Where are you?"

"Halfway up the incline!"

"Hurry!" Chad said and blew into Suzie's mouth again.

It seemed like an hour since Chad had begun, but it had to be only minutes. Suzie blinked and looked at him, this time as if she could see him. She tried to speak. He felt for a pulse. It was a little stronger, but not yet steady. She jerked and thrashed, and he thought that was a good sign. But he knew she could still die on him any second.

Chad heard two thumps on the truck and whirled to see Dad's snowshoes clatter over the hood and into the snow. He leaned out and saw Dad in the fading light at the top of the drift, a black case in both hands. Dad dove from the top and tumbled down the drift, rolling and flipping until he flopped onto the ground with a loud grunt.

Chad pushed the door open, barely missing Dad, who was reaching for the handle. "Do you have a pulse?" Dad said.

"Yes, finally."

"Suzie!" Dad called out.

She didn't respond.

"Give me the insulin," Chad said, and Dad cracked open the case, tossing aside everything that didn't say "insulin" on the label. Finally he found a vial. Chad reached past him and grabbed a hypodermic. He tore at the paper and whipped the plastic end off the needle.

Dad had just opened the vial when Chad grabbed it and held it up to the interior light. He drove the needle through the rubber opening, turned the vial upside down and, checking the gauge on the side, drew into the needle 30 units of insulin.

He pulled the needle away from the vial and let the vial fall to the floor. Pressing the plunger, he cleared the needle of air, shooting a fraction of the insulin into the air. Then he jammed the needle right through Suzie Q's snowsuit and trousers and into her inner thigh. He quickly pressed the plunger. He was surprised at how hard it was to push the liquid into her.

Chad began CPR again, but within seconds Suzie roused and began to lift her head. "Stay right there, girl," Dad said. "Stay right there."

She was groggy, but she was awake. She was breathing. Her heart was beating. Chad dropped onto the floor and sobbed.

"What happened?" Suzie said, her voice thick and her words slurred.

"Just take it easy," Dad said.

But Suzie fought to sit up. "I'm all right," she said. "Did you bring my medicine?"

"You've already gotten it," Dad said. "Chad saved your life."

"He gave me the insulin?"

"He also gave you CPR."

"He did?"

Dad nodded. Chad fought to gain control. He was spent. The CPR was one thing. But he had injected insulin into Suzie Q. And she seemed to be doing fine. He could hardly move.

Dad helped Suzie Q sit up, then pulled Chad from the floor and propped him up too. He shut the door and ran around to get behind the wheel. Suzie was breathing deeply. "I'm not going anywhere," Dad said, "especially back the same way we came, until I'm sure you're up to it."

"I feel pretty weak," she said. "But I'm up to giving Chad a hug."

"Do you have to?" Chad said.

"Yes, I do," she said. And she did.

Secretly, Chad didn't mind a bit.

Epilogue

Dad didn't attempt the drive back to the school until he was sure Suzie Q could make it. It wasn't quite as bouncy a ride this time. He followed his own tracks and drove along the path he had cleared on the way. They arrived back at the school in about half the time it had taken to travel east.

The antibiotics sped the recovery of those who were ill from what Mrs. Quenton said was an outbreak of Streptococcus pneumonia at the school. Chad was treated like a hero. This time, however, he didn't enjoy the attention. He wanted to shake the memories and the terror of Suzie Q coming so close to death right in his arms, but he knew the experience would be with him always.

Suzie Q and even Kate seemed to understand that Chad would rather not talk about the ordeal. He was grateful for that, and he changed his opinion about girls—at least those two girls.

Chad felt as if he had grown up almost overnight. He was thankful God had been with him when he needed him the most.

The Michaelses flew home a few days later, but when the roads were passable in a couple weeks, they traveled back to Old Sparrow, where Dad personally thanked his new friend, Sam, for his help. "You had as much to do with saving Sue Quenton's life as any of us did," Dad told him.

And Chad knew it was true.

He had made it through the experience of having another person's life in his hands, and Chad knew that was something he would never take lightly. This had been an incredible adventure for AirQuest Adventures—what more could the future possibly bring?

AirQuestAdventures
CRASH
at Cannibal Valley
#1 BESTSELLING AUTHOR
zonderkidz
JERRY B. JENKINS

Misery in Mukluk

Chad Michaels bounded out of Mukluk Middle School in northern Alaska. He ran as fast as he could despite his huge boots, down-filled snow pants, mittens, and hooded parka.

At noon, he and the other sixth-grade guys usually engaged in daily snowball fights against the seventh graders. Chad hated these fights; he would have skipped them if it weren't for the name-calling he'd have to endure. Today's snowball fight couldn't ruin his day though. He had two special things to look forward to that afternoon, and that's what he thought about as he ran out into the snow.

The winter sun set early in Mukluk, so the whole school was let out for recess before lunch every day. That meant there were just too many kids to watch at once, and the boys could get away with breaking the no-snowball rule. Besides, these guys had been snowball fighting for so long, they knew where to play without getting caught. Chad glanced over his shoulder. The other sixth graders were right behind him.

Chad hadn't even had time to stop and scoop up a ball of his own when he saw Rusty Testor, his least favorite seventh grader, standing a few feet away, a huge snowball in his palm. The icy wind stung Chad's exposed cheeks as he sprinted for all he was worth, but the bigger, older Testor had the angle on him and was closing fast.

Rusty had a gap-toothed, freckle-faced grin that gave Chad nightmares. *I'd love to pop him, just once*, Chad thought. He imagined himself rushing Testor, driving his head into the bigger boy's stomach, and knocking the wind right out of him. That's what his friends would do.

But not me, Chad thought as he ran. *Rusty's right. I'm a wimp.*

Chad headed for the highest, deepest drift he could find, planning to hurtle over it and fight back from the other side. But from the corner of his eye he saw Testor draw back his throwing arm. Chad mistimed his leap over the snowdrift and left the ground too early. He spread his arms and legs, but instead of flying over the top to safety, he flopped face-first into the side of the drift.

As he called to his friends for help, Rusty's snowball smacked his cheekbone and drove ice and water into his ear and eye. It burned, and he wanted to cry, but he would never do that. It was bad enough he was a klutz; he wasn't going to be a baby too. At least he wouldn't show it if he was.

Chad turned and saw Rusty scooping more ammo from about ten feet away. Several other seventh graders joined in, grinning just like Rusty. Chad squatted, covering his face with his arms and drawing up his knees to protect himself as the fusillade pummeled him.

Here was the perfect opportunity for his friends to charge the seventh graders from the rear, while they were all occupied with him. But where were they? Was he sacrificing himself for no purpose? He peeked through his hands in disbelief. They just stood outside the circle of older kids, looking at him in disgust.

"You're too easy," Rusty said. "Go hide somewhere."

Chad wanted to charge him, to throw ice balls at him, but not if his so-called friends wouldn't help. He was tired of being a sitting duck. He stood, shoulders sagging, hands at his sides, as the seventh graders turned their attention to the other sixth graders. They would put up a better fight, which was more fun for the seventh graders than terrorizing Chad.

When they trudged back into school for lunch, one of Chad's friends caught up with him. "What's the deal, Michaels? Every day it's the same thing! You're big enough, you're strong enough, you're fast enough."

AirQuestAdventures
TERROR
in Branco Grande
#1 BESTSELLING AUTHOR
JERRY B. JENKINS
zonderkidz

Women's Intuition

"You can't talk to me that way!" Kate Michaels said.

Her brother Chad sneered. "Just stop trying to act like Mom!"

Kate felt her face redden and a sob rise in her throat. She wanted to lash out, but she knew she would burst into tears. "What would be so wrong with acting like Mom?" she said. Just saying "Mom" brought back all the grief and pain of her mother's death six months before.

"Because you're not her! Nobody is or ever will be, so quit trying to be a woman or anything but a kid! And don't forget—you're not Thomas Edison, either!"

That was all Kate could take. She bounded up the steps to her room. As she flew by Dad at his desk, he said, "What are you two arguing about now?"

Kate slammed her door and flopped onto her bed. She allowed herself to cry softly, occasionally pausing to listen

for Dad. Nothing. Maybe he was already giving Chad the standard lecture about girls and their emotions. Dad was real big on their sticking together as the AirQuest Adventures team. "We're family. We're all we've got," he always said.

Kate had just started sixth grade at Mukluk Middle School in northern Alaska. She felt older and more mature than ever; sometimes she almost forgot she was almost a year younger than Chad. So if she acted like her mom sometimes, what was wrong with that?

Her mom had been killed by a drunk driver one day when they were scheduled to pick up Dad at the airport. Dad, then an Air Force fighter pilot and owner of his own charter-flight company, was returning from a military assignment.

Since their mother's death, Kate's father had retired from military work and sold the company. Dad, Chad, and Kate had then formed AirQuest Adventures, a team available to Christian organizations anywhere in the world.

Dad was the pilot, of course. Chad, who his dad liked to call Spitfire after the quick and deadly World War II plane, was the computer expert. And Kate, a techie for as long as she could remember, knew a lot about radios and communications. She had won first prize at the school science fair every year since second grade.

Recently, she'd designed a two-way wrist radio that looked like a big watch. She and Chad and Dad all had one. After school Kate had told Chad that it wouldn't take much to add a miniature high frequency band and video camera to the gadget, which would allow for a crude LCD television picture.

Chad didn't believe her, which is what had started their argument a few moments before.

"Yeah, right." Chad had laughed as he followed her into the kitchen after school. "Like we could see each other on our wrist radios."

"Why is that so hard to believe?" she said. "We have cell phones where we can see each other—and even take pictures and make video clips."

"Exactly," Chad said. "So why waste time inventing a two- or three-way radio with a TV screen?"

"Think," Kate said, rolling her eyes, "where we fly—jungles mostly—have you seen a lot of cell phone towers? Would your fancy phone be able to communicate at all?" She snorted. "You'd never pick up a signal."

Chad frowned. "True… "

Kate smiled. She loved proving him wrong. "Course, when we're talking into the radios, the other person could only see our mouth and nose, but if you held it back a ways, it would give a picture of our face or whole body."

Chad shook his head. "You're dreaming. The smallest two-way radio is ten times the size of your watch, and the smallest video camera is five times bigger than our wrist radios! How are you going to fit the machinery in there to record and send? And think of the antenna you'd need. We'd look like robots with rabbit ears!"

"You're not up on technology," Kate said. "They now make video cameras smaller than the end of your thumb. Batteries today will give you a five-mile range, and I know more than a hundred interference eliminator codes so we can hear each other clearly. Thanks to Dad, I also know the specs for military radios and what's needed to operate in harsh environments. I'm close, Chad, that's all I can say. You used to encourage me. Can't you see how it might work?"

"That's a long time away."

"No, it isn't! A Korean company has already invented a watch with a digital camera and phone. And video cameras in wristwatches already exist. I want to combine the watch and the video, but with a radio transmitter instead of a phone. The picture wouldn't be much, but it would be a start."

Chad shook his head. "It might make something interesting for this year's science fair, but you're years from making all that work."

AirQuest Adventures

Author Jerry B. Jenkins is the writer of the bestselling Left Behind novel series.

Travel 'round the world with twelve-year-old Chad, his younger sister, Kate, and their risk-taking, entrepreneur dad as the three go globe-trotting to help those in need—and land in more trouble than they ever imagined!

Crash at Cannibal Valley

ISBN 0-310-71347-1

In the first book of the AirQuest Adventures, after their plane goes down in Indonesia, Chad must help his injured sister and his dad survive in an area rumored to be inhabited by cannibals.

Terror in Branco Grande

ISBN 0-310-71346-3

The second book of the AirQuest Adventures, Dad is arrested after the AirQuest team is framed by an international smuggling ring. Kate and Chad must fight to prove Dad's innocence and escape deportation.

Available at your local bookstore!

zonderkidz

zonderkidz®

We want to hear from you. Please send your comments
about this book to us in care of zreview@zondervan.com. Thank you.

Grand Rapids, MI 49530
www.zonderkidz.com

ZONDERVAN.COM/
AUTHORTRACKER